The Adventures of June Bug Johnson

The Adventures of June Bug Johnson

GROWING UP IN THE SHADOWS OF THE
PROVERBS

Charlie Crowe

CrossLink Publishing

CrossLink Publishing
558 E. Castle Pines Pkwy, Ste B4117
Castle Rock, CO 80108
www.crosslinkpublishing.com

Ordering Information:
Quantity sales. Special discounts are available on quantity purchases by corporations, associations, and others. For details, contact the "Special Sales Department" at the address above.

The Adventures of June Bug Johnson/ Crowe —1st ed.

10 9 8 7 6 5 4 3 2 1

ISBN 978-1-63357-115-0

Library of Congress Control Number: 2017947410

All scripture quotations are taken from the Holy Bible, King James Version (Public Domain)

"The homespun wisdom and humor of Charlie Crowe's book "The Adventures of June Bug Johnson" harkens back to a different age and makes you long for the days when life seemed simpler."

Ted Huskins
Vice- President and Chief Operating Officer
Northern New England Conference

"You will fall in love with June Bug and all of the vivid characters that Charlie brings to life in his first novel."
Cindy Carland
President
Coleman Stewardship Services Inc.

Charlie Crowe's writing pulls me in to the story making me feel a part of the moment. Charlie paints the picture so I can feel, smell, taste and hear what is happening on the written page. The stories not only touch me emotionally and spiritually but they also remind me of people and times in my own life when I have had the honor and privilege to be a part of God meeting someone at the point of their greatest need. June Bug Johnson and Grandpa Lymon will entertain you, comfort you, inspire you and encourage you to keep on moving even in the tough times. You deserve to be uplifted by this book.
Mike Winsor,
Chaplain, BSW, MM, NACC, Chairman CRM

"Good story telling, I could picture the scene clearly in my mind as I read this and it drew me in. The lesson behind the story was well done and right on point. Enjoyed this very much."
Ray Holloway
Operator Chick-fil-a at Archer Rd. Gainesville FL

However the news of the day comes to you, radio, TV, newsprint or streamed, it is mostly depressing. The burden of a day's activities can be overwhelming. So, a few minutes reading a chapter of The Adventures of June Bug Johnson may be what the Doctor wanted you to have. The stories presented are of a simpler time and place, light-hearted but containing a message needed in today's world.

Life lessons taught in a way in which they can be enjoyed and appreciated. Try it, I think you might like it.
David Chapman,
Consultant Kairos Legacy Partners

"I've always thought Charlie was good at telling stories. Now that I've read about June Bug, I know he is! If you grew up in the American South, you'll see a bit of yourself in June Bug's adventures and misadventures, and hopefully, you'll learn something, too."
Michael Moebes,
Attorney at Law

Folksy and down home. American by birth, southern by the grace of God. These descriptions and anecdote dovetail perfectly with, "The Adventures of June Bug Johnson." I'm usually not much of a reader, but this was surprisingly enjoyable. Maybe it's because I'm a Southern boy at heart, or maybe it's just June Bug Johnson is so easy to relate to. Either way, I highly recommend it. Two thumbs up!
Tim Spivey,
Minister High Springs Church of Christ

With a wit akin to Dave Barry, a tone that matches the late Lewis Grizzard, and wisdom similar to Reverend Will B. Dunn, the author tells tales that are clearly close to his heart and his funny bone. The stories will charm the young and young at heart, saints and sinners, and the grumpy and the joyous. Some stories will result in an uncontrollable guffaw, others a sly smile and occasionally, yes even a sentimental tear. This is a book for all who believe in the great beauty of heart and head coming together as one.

Jeff Welch,
Pastor Dunnellon Presbyterian Church

Charlie Crowe's homespun southern humor makes for a delightful read! The characters from The Adventures of June Bug Johnson offer a good laugh and precious life lessons.

David Welsh,
Senior Minister Franklin Christian Church, Franklin TN

Mr. Crowe's stories have the appeal and charm of a by–gone era, reminiscent of the safe–yet–quirky world of Mayberry. He is able to miraculously create in readers a nostalgia for a time and place they have most likely never known––no small feat. Much like the writings of Annie Dillard, Mr. Crowe is also able to reveal how the Holy Spirit manifests itself in the mundane and everyday existence where most of us only find sterility and darkness.

DJ DYCUS, PH.D.
PROFESSOR OF ENGLISH AND HUMANITIES
Point University

Mr. Crowe combines wisdom and humor In The Adventures of June Bug Johnson. Each story, fit for a 21st century Book of Virtues, will leave you laughing while being able to relate to the characters in the story. My favorite story was "The Worst Whipping in the History of McComb County" where young James Worth learns a painful lesion about bad influences but I won't spoil the ending, read it for yourself.

Abigail Havens
IC2(SW) United States Navy

The Adventures of June Bug Johnson is a fresh new take on Solomon's classic proverbs. Children and adults alike will be able to take away important life lessons after seeing these Biblical texts through real world lenses. And best of all, my son just thought it was «too much fun!» It is a great addition to any homeschooler's collection.

Elise Hill,
homeschool mom of three

The Adventures of June Bug Johnson is a wholesome, humorous series of stories that the whole family will adore! Life in the Southern Heartland reminisces of a simpler time when faith and family came first. I look forward to reading and rereading this to my children for years to come.

-Mrs. Ghizzoni,
mother of two

The Adventures of June Bug Johnson Growing up in the Shadow of the Proverbs is a must read! With a modern day twist from wisdom out of the Proverbs that is brought to real life by the experience of a small, back-hills, country boy, this book will have you laughing, crying, and even asking God about your own life all at the same time.

Reverend Jennifer F. Beagle
Women's Director, House of Hope

This book combines classic southern story-telling with Biblical truth. Only the Lord could have foreseen Solomon's wisdom applied in such a humorous manner in the deep South. You'll laugh with a purpose as you meet colorful characters with grit, grace, or neither.

Jim Bob McAllister
President KEYSYS Inc.

To my grandchildren: "Let me tell you a story"

To my children: "Thank you for making it possible"

Contents

Hope is the preferred vision of the future.

Nostalgia is the preferred vision of the past.

Acknowledgments

Lorie: Thank you for being one of the heroes of the story of my life; oh and thanks for your faithful support and help with this project. Without you the stories of June Bug would have never progressed beyond the ramblings of a story teller.

To my family and friends: Thank you for letting me tell you stories, jokes, and painful puns. Hold up a finger for every time you have heard this story.

Introduction

Once upon a time there was a place filled with wonder, amazement, excitement, beauty, fear, adventure, heroic selflessness, and on many occasions, remarkable stupidity. This place was a great place to grow up; this place was called childhood. The problem with childhood is that you have no clue what you are doing or how to do it. Thankfully, God gives us some great guides to help us through the wanderings of youth. Among those guides are our elders, folks who have lived through their own folly and can help us learn from their experiences. When we are young our elders seem so wise and so secure that we feel they could never have made a mistake out of sheer stupidity. But when they were young, they too had a tendency to slip into folly. Because of that, they can tell about *their* experiences with folly. We can travel back in time by means of the marvel of story.

A story can be a time machine. In a well-told story we are able, at least in our minds, to travel back in time to a place where we have never been. We may not interact with the events, but in our imagination, we can be eyewitnesses to momentous happenings. There is something about hearing a story that makes a person smarter; that is, if we are listening. Some stories are pure history and fact, where everything that is told is an exact representation of the events as they transpired. Sometimes stories are purely made-up. There is not a word about them that actually happened. Some stories are a historic fact with a few interesting exaggerations added to liven it up a bit. We have to tell the truth and nothing but the truth when asked for the truth, but a story, if we know it is a story, we can enjoy for what it is.

In the Bible, we see both history and stories. It is important that we are careful to understand the difference. The "Prodigal Son" is a story; the Flood of Noah is a history. Generally, it is not too hard to tell the difference. As a guide for wisdom, there is nothing that can compare with the Word of God. Our Father has been around a long time and has seen a lot of history and He has told us more than a few stories. In the book of Proverbs, He has given us a marvelous amalgamation of history and story. Each one of the Proverbs is a little story in itself. If you read the Proverbs with your imagination wide open, you can almost see the events of each story that prompted each Proverb. You get the idea that each time Solomon penned one of the proverbs he was thinking about someone.

The Adventures of June Bug Johnson is these three themes weaving themselves together as a boy learns a little wisdom in a world of folly. All of these stories in these pages have, at their root, a story told to me as true; and all of the stories have been embellished, some a little and some a lot. I did this to add a little flavor to the story and to protect the identity of the characters. I have no intention of telling how much embellishment happened and to which stories. But some folks still living might recognize a flicker of their past. I took a lot of stories, added some made-up details and put them into the life of one fictional character.

These stories are unabashedly and unashamedly nostalgic. But as the saying goes, "Nostalgia isn't what it used to be." We tend to remember the good old days better than they actually were. A friend of mine who grew up during the depression used to say, "I clearly remember the good 'ole days and they were miserable."

Hope has been defined as, "our preferred vision of the future, consistent with the noblest aspiration of our faith." We might say that nostalgia is, "the preferred vision of our past, reflecting our most cherished values and sentiment." What hope is to the future, nostalgia is to the past. Our memory is not clear, indeed, it is perhaps not very accurate at all, but in nostalgia we are able to see those things that are good, noble and heroic, and heart-warming and winsome. By using a nostalgic lens to view these proverbs, hopefully, it will bring into clear relief what matters in our lives.

In a world that is growing in folly daily, we desperately need to learn the wisdom of the Proverbs. We need to see these as more than ancient sayings, but rather as the story of life. It is my fervent hope that you will see in June Bug's adventures how utterly practical and joyful is the wisdom of God.

In the Cause of Christ,
Charlie Crowe

CHAPTER 1

Worst Klan Rally Ever

McComb County was unique in that the racial tensions that swept the South during the civil rights movements were not so intense there. That is not to say that there were none, but it never got so ugly as it did in other places. Lots of folks from McComb, both black and white, would say it was because they were just a bit brighter and just better than other folks. Some would say it was because McComb County was far enough off the beaten path that outside agitators had never found their way there. But the truth was that racial tensions were muted in McComb County because of two men, Horace Jones and Lymon Baker.

Pastor Horace Jones was a very kind, brilliant man who pastored the Great Pisgah AME Church in McComb County and he was the voice of the blacks or, as they were often called, "colored" folks. Brother Jones was a big man standing a spot over 6 feet, 6 inches tall. He had a long face the color of ebony which made his smile, which he always seemed to wear, that much brighter. He was not a firebrand kind of preacher, but one who would talk you in to what was right. It was said he could talk the legs off a mule and still get it to go for a walk. His deep, rich, baritone voice, which must have sounded like God's own voice, might not calm a storm, but it would take control of a situation and soothe a rowdy crowd. It wasn't that he couldn't get loud; he just didn't need to. To look at him, he appeared to be a long, lanky, clumsy fellow. But he was actually graceful and even elegant, especially when he played the piano. Brother Jones had a way with people; even folks who didn't like him were somehow drawn to him.

The black folks had Brother Jones and the white folks had Lymon (pronounced Lemon) Baker. Lymon was a Godly man, but not a minister. He ran a general store, which carried most anything you might need. Lymon loved his store, but he knew that general stores were slowly fading away. They were, like so many old traditions, becoming a thing of the past by the late '50's and early '60's. In big towns like Montgomery, there were department stores that were several stories tall. But the difference between a big department store and a general store was more than size.

Lymon felt that the real value of a store was the friendship between the customer and the shopkeeper. He would treat a man with a $75 order no different than a child buying a penny candy, except that he would occasionally give the candy away. Lymon loved people and the general store was just a way to be around people. When taking an order, he would let folks talk as long as they needed; both by disposition and habit, he did not rush. Among the shelves of canned meats, chewing tobacco, string, pistol and rifle cartridges, the one thing folks came for most was the friendship. If Lymon didn't have what a customer wanted, he would order it for 'em, at no extra charge.

Ice boxes, as they were called then, with cold Cokes, Pepsi, Nehi, Peach Pop or root beers sat in front of the counter and within easy reach of the ice boxes were the rockers. In the heat of summer folks would move to the front porch and in the coldest of winter they moved near the old stove. The wood floor under the rockers was worn smooth from years of faithful use and it was rare that the rockers were ever empty. Mostly the men too old to work sat and rocked, whittling and occasionally spitting amber. But if a lady came in, the men would get up to offer a seat to her, and the same was true if a youngster was sitting and his elder walked in. In a lot of ways, Lymon's store was everybody's second home.

Lymon was fond of quoting from the Good Book, telling stories and laughing. He was different than many store owners of that time in that he treated whites and blacks just the same. He didn't have the education of some folks, but he had a sense of humor better than most. Horace and Lymon became friends the day they meet, but never made a big deal about it. You know how some white folks would say, "I'm friends with black people," to act like they weren't racist. Horace and Lymon weren't like that, they were just friends. As I was saying, they became friends the day they met.

Brother Jones had just moved to McComb County to take the ministry at Great Pisgah. He was recommended to this church 'cause he had cousins attending there. It was a Saturday and he came to the store to get something. As he walked in Bud Watson, one of the no-count, white trash Watson's, knowing he was new in the area decided to try to have some fun. He said, "Hey, boy, don't you know you are supposed to use the back door?"

Lymon stepped up at that moment and said, "Bud, you know the rule in my store, freight in the backdoor, customers in the front door, and no counts and Tennessee Vols fans use the side door" (The store didn't have a side door). "So, if you don't want to be stuck on the outside, you watch your mouth. This is my new best customer." From that day on Brother Jones liked Lymon. It was reported that when things got really tense with the Civil Rights Movement, they would meet every Monday early in the morning and pray for McComb County. The only character flaw Lymon ever found in Horace was he was a Tennessee Vols fan. Lymon was fond of saying, "I cut myself one time and, low and behold, I bled Crimson." Next to his love for God, Lymon loved football and that meant the Alabama Crimson Tide.

No one in Lymon Baker's hearing ever said anything ill of Horace unless it had to do with his being a Vols fan. But when it came to football, Lymon and Horace teased each other without mercy. Lymon even threatened to require Horace to use the side door for the whole week before the big game every year. This teasing wasn't limited to Lymon. Horace's own congregation would pick on him pretty hard about being on the wrong side of right and wrong when it came to football.

In 1962, the Ku Klux Klan had been making noise all over and they were calling for a march and a protest everywhere they could. The only active Klansmen in McComb County lived way up on the north end of the county and they generally did their stuff in bigger places, in the counties just north of McComb. They came down once and organized a Klan coven in south McComb and instructed them to have a march. This wasn't much of an organization. It was made up of Max Hardy, Bud Watson, his boy Arnan (a name they had picked out of the Bible), and Harry Chestnut.

The Hardy family had been in McComb County since before the war (When a southern says "the war" they are, of course, referring the war of Northern Aggression or what Yankees call the Civil War). The Hardy family was once a powerful and prominent family, but a few generations of spoiled children had diffused and wasted the family fortune. The Hardy's were, for the most part, bad people, dishonest in business, mean-spirited and difficult to be around. A few of the Hardy's still had some land or business interest, but they weren't the cat's whiskers they thought they were.

The Watson's were pure, no count, ornery, white-trash. There was hardly a vice known to man that was not the practice of one or another of the Watson's. They were almost universally lazy, shiftless and poor. Very few Watson's escaped the heritage of poverty and ignorance that was the hallmark of that family. The Watson's had always been poor, and when they did work; it was generally in the employ of one of the Hardy families. As such, they were beholden to the Hardy's. The Hardy's looked down on the Watson's and put on airs that they were their betters, but there really wasn't much difference between 'em. Someone said, "The difference between a Watson and a Hardy is a Watson displays his sin in public; a Hardy does it behind closed doors." It was to the point that the Watson's were about the only folks that would have anything to do with the Hardy's.

Harry Chestnut was not related to either family. Harry was slow, or as some would say, retarded. His mama was a good, hard-working lady, but his daddy ran off when Harry was little. Harry was a loveable child in a man's body. He had 'graduated' from school, not because he had passed the classes, but because he couldn't stay in school forever and folks loved him too much to fail him out. He lived with his mama and did odd jobs now and again. But, mostly, Harry spent his time just being Harry, liking people and wanting to be liked. Harry wouldn't hurt a fly, but Arnan Watson, pretending to be his friend, began to try to teach him to talk ugly and say racist things. But he really didn't understand what he was doing. It was Arnan that convinced Harry that he should join the KKK. Arnan would tell him to do things and Harry would just do as he was told. Max didn't like having Harry as part of their Klan; he said he made them look dumb.

Bud said, "We'll keep him around till we get built up a little and then get shed of him."

They would meet every so often and act like a big, important, secret organization. Problem was Harry could not keep a secret and would tell anybody who asked-and some folks who didn't-all about their secret plans. That is why, when they announced the "South McComb County Knights of the Ku Klux Klan March," it was no big news. Everybody in the community knew about it because Harry had been bragging that he was going to get to carry the KKK flag.

Their plan was to have a massive march down to Lymon's General Story, Max would make a speech and then they would recruit new members. All the Klansmen were to keep their faces covered except for Max because he was making a speech. Harry wanted to make a speech too. But he was told his job of holding the flag was too important to be distracted by speeching. Harry was kind of getting tired of being in the Klan 'cause it mostly amounted to doing whatever Arnan told him to do. For example, Harry wasn't sure why he had to wash Arnan's car if they weren't going to drive it to the march. But Arnan said he outranked Harry; so, Harry was told he had to do it and Harry reluctantly did it.

Now the schedule for the Klan march was not well planned. They planned the March for the third Saturday in October, which meant it was the same day as the Alabama-Tennessee football game. Now given the choice of listening to Max Hardy make a Klan speech or listening to the Alabama game most folks, white and black, would choose to listen to the Bama game. This was a special Alabama-Tennessee game because it was the first one where Lymon would be listening to it with his new grandson, Deroy Johnson Jr (who later would become known as June Bug, among other things). June Bug was going to be there; he was in diapers and didn't really care about football yet, but he was going to be there all the same. For his part Lymon, who adopted the title Grandpa Lymon on this day, was thrilled. As always, he would open the store to any who would care to come and listen to the broadcast of the game on his radio.

Folks would arrive early and talk about the game and generally socialize. Among those who were there was Brother Jones. Bama was a heavy favorite, but Brother Jones was a faithful fan even if his team was having a down year. What with the excitement of the game and the presence of the new baby, Grandpa Lymon was in rare form, having fun and laughing.

Folks generally forgot about the KKK march, till the four of 'em started walking toward the store porch. A good crowd of people stood around the porch, blacks and whites, and watched as they walked-they were not in step enough to be a march-up to the porch.

What happened next showed that Lymon had not forgotten about the march and was expecting 'em. Max cleared his throat to get ready to make his speech or at least let folks know he was going to make a speech. Before he got started Grandpa Lymon stepped down to the four of 'em and reached in his pocket. Folks got a little tense 'cause everyone knew how Lymon felt about the KKK.

Well, Lymon put his hand in this pocket and pulled out four sticks of hard candy and says real loud, "Now children it is a bit early for Halloween, but you put in a good effort to dress like ghosties so I'll give you a bit of candy." The four of 'em were so shocked they just took the candy as Lymon handed it to them and then stood there stock-still-all except Harry. He drawls out, "Thank you, Mr. Baker," and takes off his hood so he can taste the candy. It was at this point that most of the white folks laughed out loud and the black folks guffawed under their breath.

When Arnan saw this, he backhanded Harry on the arm and said, "Put your hood on so no one will know who we are."

Harry was more interested in the candy than the hood and, in fumbling with the candy, he dropped the KKK flag.

Arnan yelled, "Pick that up! You disgrace our flag."

Harry yelled back, "You pick it up. I'm tired of carrying it."

Then Arnan shoved Harry real hard and causes him to drop his candy stick. Well, Harry started to cry a little and saying Arnan had to get him another stick of candy. Arnan was yelling for Harry to do what he was told 'cause everybody there out ranks him. Harry says he don't want to be in the Klan no more and they can keep their secrets and their robes and their flag.

As they started yelling and shoving, Lymon stepped up and said, "Harry, you take off that silly robe and you can come listen to the game with the rest of us and I'll give you another stick of candy."

Harry may have been slow, but he could make a decision quick. He was out of the robe and up the steps in a heartbeat. And folks started moving into the store, because it was almost time for kick-off. Lymon looked back at the three in the street standing there with the flag at their feet and still holding their candy sticks.

He said to 'em, "Get rid of them robes and we will welcome you to come in and listen to the game."

Bud said some things I won't repeat and then said, "Arnan, pick up the flag and extra robe and let's go."

"Why do I have to carry it?" Arnan defiantly asked.

"Cause I outrank you!" This began a loud conversation about who did outrank the other.

Brother Jones was the picture of dignity through it all, even with Bama beating the Vols 35 to 0. For Grandpa Lymon it was nearly a perfect day, what with Deroy "June Bug" Johnson Jr.'s first trip to listen to a game at the general store and Bama winning big on the third Saturday in October. Harry left the KKK, though he still had to unlearn some of the things he was taught by Arnan, but folks were patient with him. Harry even started being friends with Brother Jones and would occasionally attend services at Great Mt. Pisgah AME Church.

The Klan never was strong in that part of the county. People always have to deal with their own hates and all, but it seemed that the KKK never recovered from the worst Klan rally in history.

CHAPTER 2

Leaning in and Falling Back, June Bug Learns About the Fear of God

O ne Sunday riding home from church, June Bug was talking to Grandpa Lymon about the service and what different things in the sermon meant. When they passed the Watson place there was a deputy's car out in the yard. Nadab Watson or some of his clan were at it again. Most likely someone spent Saturday night drinking, got up about noon and had a fracas with another family member.

It usually started with a white trash screaming match, spilled out onto the front yard and then somebody would hit, or threaten to hit, somebody else and it would end up with a call to the sheriff. And now Deputy Billy "Cooter" Harris was pointing with his left index finger, yelling something to Nadab Watson with his right hand on his nightstick. It looked like he might need to get it out and smack it upside Mr. Watson's head. Mr. Watson was all red faced and cussing (you couldn't hear what he was saying, but if'n he was mad and he said anything, it was a cuss). He was about five feet from Cooter acting like a little bantam rooster, strutting around and puffing up his chest.

Cooter wouldn't mind much smacking old Nadab Watson. Cooter was a big man about six feet tall and going on 215 pounds. He had served a hitch in the Army as a M.P. then came back home to McComb County and went to work in the Sheriff's office. Most of the time Cooter was really a very sweet, easygoing fellow; the kind of law man who gave more warnings than speeding tickets. But he didn't like the Watson's. He had had enough experience with the Watson's to not trust any of 'em at all. Ever since 7th grade Cooter had been looking for a reason to bust that old, no count, drunk, white-trash a good one.

Back in 7th grade, Cooter was good friends with Betty Watson, Nadab's only daughter. One day Betty came to school with a busted lip and a black eye. She told everybody she got hurt playing football with her brother and cousin Arnan. But during recess she was sitting by herself and Cooter came up and asked if she wanted to swing or something. She just shook her head "no." That is when Cooter saw a tear on her cheek.

Cooter asked, "Betty, what's wrong?"

Betty looked up and both her eyes are full of tears and she said, "My daddy hits me when he drinks," and she just hung her head.

Cooter, only 13 years old, had no idea what to do, so he just said, "I am sorry, Betty, I really am." They never said another word about it, but from that day on Cooter had thought about hitting Nadab Watson on many an occasion.

Well, as Grandpa Lymon and June Bug rode by you could hear old Cooter yelling, "Get your hands out where I can see 'em our I'll...." The rest of what he said was lost in the noise of the wind blowing in the window.

Grandpa Lymon didn't change his expression at all; he just did what he always did when he felt really strong about something, he quoted from the book of Proverbs: "The fear of the LORD is the beginning of knowledge: but fools despise wisdom and instruction."

"What does that mean, Grandpa?" June Bug asked without being really precise

"It means Nadab Watson is about to get his head busted open and Billy Harris is going to spend the afternoon filling out a report." Grandpa said without much inflection in his voice.

"Grandpa, the 'fear of the Lord' part, I hear you and momma and daddy and the preacher talk about 'love and fear God'. I ain't speaking ill of the Good Book, but fear and love don't seem to go together. What does that mean?"

Grandpa Lymon sat really quiet as he drove. He sat quiet so long June Bug was beginning to think he was in trouble. Finally, about the time they were getting to the house for Sunday dinner Grandpa Lymon finally broke the silence, "I don't think I can explain it; I will have to show you."

June Bug was getting scared now thinking this might be a whipping coming for speaking ill of the Good Book or the Lord or something. "Am I in trouble, Grandpa, 'cause if I said something I wasn't supposed to I didn't go to." (If you said 'Go to' it was a declaration of intent. "He knocked you down, but he didn't 'go to' {mean to}).

"You're not in trouble, son. You are never in trouble for wanting to understand God, but some things are easier shown than told."

When they got to the house, Grandpa Lymon walked in and hugged his daughter like he hadn't seen her in ten years, even though he had just been at church with her 20 minutes ago. "Caroline, I need you to write a note to June Bug's school; tell them he will be out tomorrow. I need to take him somewhere. I am going to learn him something."

"Why sure, where you going?"

Now these were the days when schools understood that parents were supposed to be in charge of what their children did. If a parent wanted to take a child out of school and the parent thought it was for a good cause the parent did it and the school didn't mind. Of course, back then parents would also make sure that their child would get his studies done. Now, Grandpa Lymon really didn't need a note. He was so well known and respected he could have just gone and gotten June Bug, but that wouldn't have been fittin'.

"I'm going to take June Bug to the place where I learned what it meant to fear the Lord."

June Bug's head was spinning. In five minutes, he had gone from being pretty sure he was going to get a whippin', to finding out he would skip a day of school and spend it going who-knows-where with Grandpa Lymon. All through lunch he asked Grandpa where he was going, but got not a bit of an answer; could not even get a hint or clue.

After lunch, mama ruined all the fun by calling June Bug's teacher and getting some of June Bugs assignments. Sunday afternoon was when June Bug would normally go play, swim, watch football or do something fun, but this Sunday he had to spend it doing school. But he didn't mind too much in view of getting out of school the next day.

Next morning earlier than most Mondays, June Bug's mama woke him and told him to get up for breakfast. When he came to the kitchen Grandpa Lymon was sitting there dressed like it was Sunday or at the least market day. "Morning, son, you ready to go to the mountains?" Grandpa said as if this day was like any other.

"Yes sir," and June Bug headed for the door.

"Not till you eat, young man," Mama said.

This had to be a special day 'cause mama fixed Johnny cakes, pancakes made with cornmeal. Most mornings, mama fixed something fast and easy, but nothing like this.

"So, where we going?" June Bug says.

"Caroline, have this boy's hearing checked when we get back. I just said we was going to the mountains and did you hear that question he just asked me?" Grandpa said with a twinkle in his eye and a mischievous smile just waiting to come out.

McComb County is in the flat lands; what some people call LA, Lower Alabama. There are a few hills and knolls, but not a lot of elevation change. To go to the mountains you have to head north and east. For several hours, that is just what they did. But time passes fast when you ride with Grandpa Lymon. He told stories-some June Bug had heard, some were new, all were interesting. He heard for the first time the story of the worst Klan rally in the history of the KKK. He heard the story about Cline Baker, a distant kin, who got shot by his dog. There was serious talk about Grandmother Baker who died when June Bug's daddy, Deroy, was a boy. The passage of time was only marked by June Bug's grumbling stomach.

Finally, they began twisting and turning on steep roads that always seemed to go up hill. They were climbing to the highest point in the state of Alabama, Mt Cheeha. June Bug's ears popped and his eyes bugged out as they traveled around a curve and he could see down into a valley. At last, they reached the top and pulled up to the tower built during the Depression that stood on the highest point of the state. Grandpa Lymon and June Bug climbed to the tower's top and took in the view. For a boy that had never been on a hill bigger than nothing, words failed to describe his experience. He felt like he could just jump out of the window of the tower and fly all the way to Mississippi. When he said that, Grandpa Lymon said, "You feel that way 'cause of that railing you are leaning on. Let's go eat that lunch your mama packed for us."

They got the picnic out of the bed of the truck and Grandpa Lymon led off down a trail with June Bug carrying the picnic. They walked a good ways when June Bug asked, "What has all this got to do with fearing God?" All Grandpa Lymon said was, "You will see."

They came out of the pines to a rocky spot. It was a big slab of rock that went off to nothing. It was like the view from the tower, but more open. There was one big rock that Grandpa Lymon said was called "Pulpit Rock". Grandpa said, "Beautiful ain't it?"

"Yes, sir, most beautiful thing I have ever seen."

Grandpa Lymon said, "Come on up to the edge."

So, June Bug started walking up to the edge of the cliff and looked over. When he got about five feet from the edge he stopped.

"Go on, boy, skooch up to the edge." Grandpa Lymon said from behind.

June Bug shuffled his feet another few inches. Grandpa Lymon in a voice that was light and happy as if there wasn't a care in the world said, "Go on boy, get up where you can see over."

"Sir, I can see over from here," June Bug said.

"June Bug, get up there where your toes is hanging over that cliff and look down."

Try as he might he could not move any closer than within about two feet of the edge. Matter of fact, June Bug was getting pretty close to tears with the terror that was coming up inside of him. "Grandpa, I don't want to get no closer."

Grandpa said, "Let's try this. We will lay down on our bellies and craw up and look over." That is what they did. Laying there looking over the edge, they could see Red-tailed Hawks circling below them, huge trees from the top side and cars on distant roads that looked like ants. After lying there for a moment, Grandpa Lymon said, "I'm hungry. Let's eat."

Seated back from the cliff in the shade of a pine tree, they ate a picnic big enough for three working men. Mama used this occasion to clean out a few leftovers and since mama was a great cook this was no bad thing. They had Johnny cakes from that morning, fried chicken from Sunday dinner, 'tater salad, baked ham, crackers, two moon pies and a thermos of buttermilk. I am getting a bit hungry just talking about it. While they were eating June Bug asked, "Is that what it means to fear God? Being up next to the cliff like I was?"

Grandpa Lymon swished his buttermilk around, swallowed and said, "First of On the one hand, you said this was the most beautiful thing you had ever seen, but on the other hand, it scared you really bad. When a person learns what God is like, he can't help but love Him because he understands how wondrous God is. But at the same time it is like the edge of the cliff, with the beauty is also the fear. So, when He is close you want to fall down in front of Him. God is too big to explain this way, but it may help you learn to love and fear God."

After they finished eating, June Bug went back up to the edge of the cliff. He never could stand right at the edge. He felt like the best place to be was on his knees. Grandpa Lymon knelt by him and said, "When love and fear meet, your knees are the best place to be."

They sat out by pulpit rock and talked on about God and family and the beauty of creation. After a bit, Grandpa Lymon said, "It's time to go, son. Take another look and let's be off." June Bug eased close to the edge of the cliff, took it all in and then ran and grabbed his grandpa's hand and headed home.

Oh, and by the way, Nadab Watson did try something. He was drunk enough to be too sure of himself, so he pulled a knife on Deputy Harris. Cooter swung his baton and hit Watson across the knuckles, broke a couple of bones and put him in a cast. Nadab claimed it was police brutality and even brought a case. Didn't go over too well at the hearing. The judge appointed to review the evidence concluded, "In the opinion of this court, Nadab Watson was stupid and deserved more than a busted hand. This case is dismissed."

CHAPTER 3

The Worst Whipping in the History of McComb County

Not all the Watson's are no-count white trash. Some, even most of them, are. They keep busy spending all their time and money up to no good. Some of them are about half trash. They can hold a steady job and keep themselves pretty decent most of the time, but occasionally get messed up in some kind of nefarious wickedness. But one family among all the Watson's made it out of the trap of trashy living. It was a long process, but the straw that broke the camel's back happened right in front of June Bug.

Betty Watson was a real looker when she was a girl. She was real smart and made good grades all the way through school. She wanted to go to college, but her daddy, Nadab Watson, was opposed to her getting an education. He said, "A woman ought to mind her place and home and not worry about no book learning." But he wasn't a sexist; he felt that way about boys going to college as well.

He told her, "Why don't you go get a job at the truck stop and see if you can't get some man to marry up with you. While you work you might get a husband out of the deal." His plan was for her to marry a man who wouldn't be around much, so she would live at home and he would charge her rent. Now he was pure white trash.

She did meet a trucker and married him. Turns out he was a handsome young man from near Meridian Mississippi named Douglas Worth. Doug was a good man and took good care of Betty. He got her a place of her own away from her family. He encouraged her to get a better job than waiting tables at a truck stop.

That is how she got a job with the school board. Plenty of the folks there knew she was really bright and were hoping she might get back in school. Betty and Doug had a baby about the same time June Bug was born and they named him James Longstreet Worth. In the Watson family, most of the boys were named after a Bible character or a Confederate general. Betty and Doug tried to keep James from being around the Watson's clan too much. They were family, but they were a bad influence. By and large, James was getting on pretty good. His daddy was gone a lot, but was home almost every weekend. When Doug was home he worked really hard at being a good daddy to little Jim, and Betty worked hard to make sure he did not grow up like most Watsons. Working at the school board, his mama would find out if James did the least thing wrong, which he occasionally did, and Betty would correct matters really quick. James was one of the best behaved children in the school.

After James had finished the 3rd grade, his momma got a job offer over near Montgomery that was really good. It had a lot to offer, but it also meant that James would have to stay with someone each evening until she got in from work. Doug suggested they let James stay with her family. He knew they were bad, but he didn't really understand how bad they could be. Betty was not sure about this idea at all. She was afraid James would pick up on some of the white-trashy ways of the Watson's. Doug promised her at the first sign of trouble they would make other arrangements.

So just before 4th grade, James began spending his days with his Pappy Watson. During the school year, James' mama would take him to her dad's and James would ride the bus to school, come back to Pappy Watson's and stay there until Betty picked him up late in the evening. The bad influence was immediate, but the first sign of trouble did not show up for several months.

James had been a good student, but in 4th grade he was different. He was mouthy and always on the edge of getting into trouble. He sat beside June Bug in the third period and June Bug noticed he was different. June Bug told his mama how James was acting and all she would say was, "You mind yourself and don't do anything that would get YOU in trouble with him." Some folks said that the apple didn't fall far from the tree and that James was half-Watson and the trash was just starting to come out.

June Bug agreed with James about one thing. They both hated "Journal Time". Mrs. Green, the 4th grade teacher, required the students to spend some time every day writing in a journal. They had to fill up one page with "original thoughts and reflections on what they felt was important" as Mrs. Green would put it. June Bug felt like it was stupid and said, "I don't have a page worth of thoughts every day." James also hated journal time and one day spent the whole page writing about how stupid it was. Despite the protests, every day Mrs. Green in a perky voice would say, "Students, get out your journals and fill a page with creativity."

One Friday morning, James was in an especially bad mood (these were becoming more frequent) and when journal time came he began to fill the page, not with words, but with a drawing. Now, as I tell you this story, remember that James would have never thought of this, nor even conceived of it before he started spending so much time with his Watson kin. James began to draw a picture of Mrs. Green, but he drew the picture with her naked. There was no doubt who James was drawing-the big glasses, the pointed nose, the beehive hairdo-it was Mrs. Green.

But just in case anyone missed the point, James captioned the picture in bold letters, F*** MRS GREEN.

With the picture done, James said in a whisper that was louder than he expected, "PSSST, June Bug, looky here." June Bug looked up and audibly gasped. Well, between the, "psst" and gasp, Mrs. Green came over and picked up James' notebook and looked at herself in obscene art. James knew what was coming so he got up and headed to the hall for a paddling. He had gotten so many this year that he knew what to do. Once in the hall, Mrs. Green knocked on the door of the next classroom to call for the teacher. It was Mrs. Mac. She was mean as a snake and about was wide as a Sherman tank. She was universally despised by everyone except the other teachers, parents, administrators, and her former students. Mrs. Mac came out into the hall to witness the paddling. In those days, a teacher could whip a child but they had to have a witness. Mrs. Mac had witnessed James get several paddlings and so after two licks she asked, "What did he do this time?" Mrs. Green held the journal up for Mrs. Mac to see. Mrs. Mac's eyes got really big for a second; she looked at James and then without a word she snatched the paddle out of Mrs. Green's hand and popped James two times really hard herself.

James went back into the classroom and got a good case of the sulks just sitting in his seat and waiting for P.E. class the next period. It was a cold, rainy day, so for P.E. the kids went down to the gym to play dodgeball, kick ball or some other game. Just before P.E. was over, the gym door swung open really hard and made a big racket. All the kids turned to see what was happening. There in the door way was someone who looked a lot like James' mama, except this woman had a red face with smoke coming out of her nostrils and fire spurting out of her eyes. This woman didn't say a word, just pointed at James and gestured with her whole arm indicating that she wanted him to come over to where she was.

As soon as James got near, her arm flashed out like a rattlesnake and grabbed him by the upper arm and commenced to drag him down the hall. The first door she came to was the girl's bathroom, so in they went. There was a little girl in there washing her hands and this woman that had James by the arm and kinda looked like Betty Worth tells the girl, "Get out." When that door closed behind the little girl the beating began. James, for his part, tried to run, but his mama was his anchor and so all James did was run in a circle while his mama wailed on him. She hit him forehand, backhand, uppercut, ball fist, open hand slap. You would have a hard time naming a form of bare-hand beating that Betty Worth didn't use on James. All the while, James was running and screaming and calling out that she was going to kill him. Finally, James yelled out, "Call the police, call the police – she is going to kill me." His mama never let up on him.

The only thing she said (it wasn't to James, but almost to herself or maybe to the bathroom walls), "In this county, they don't call the police when one white trash Watson beats on another. If he is going act like a white trash Watson I will treat him like one."

James claimed that the whipping lasted over an hour, but it didn't even last 'til the end of P.E. But it was a world class beating all the same. It seemed that James' mama had worked up a good head of steam in the amount of time it took her to get the call from the school, drive the 45 minutes to the school and find James. Well, she dragged James back down the hallway and pushed him into the gym and walked off without another word.

June Bug saw James walk in his face red with hand marks on it, crying and snotting and unable to talk. June Bug walked over and said, "At least you don't have to wait 'til you go home to get whipped. That is something, I suppose." June Bug was never known for being a prognosticator. Because when James got home, his daddy was waiting for him. He didn't always get in early on Friday, but on this, of all days, he was at Pappy Watson's when James got there. James didn't even go in the house; he just got in the car and headed home.

Once they got there Doug said, "Foolishness is bound up in the heart of a child but the rod of correction shall drive it far from him."

James asked, "Does this mean you goin' whip me too?"

"I am afraid so, son," and Doug whipped him, but of the four whippings that day it was the easiest to endure. Then Doug hugged James and said, "Son, your mama loves you very much, but she is afraid, bad afraid."

"What she afraid of, Daddy?"

"She is afraid that you are turning into something that she hates and she is so scared she is beside herself. And when your mama gets afraid she gets really angry."

About that time Betty came in and you could tell she had been crying. She ran over and grabbed James and hugged on him and started crying. She told him, "I love you, son, and I am sorry. I am going to make sure this kind of thing never happens again. We got some changes to make."

She then walked over to the phone, picks it up and calls someone. "Sheriff's office, this is Betty Worth. I need to get a message to Deputy Billy Harris. Tell him I need him to meet me at my daddy's place at 8:30. Yes that is right, Nadab Watson's place. Thank you."

Doug asked, "Baby, what you doing?"

"Telling Daddy that James will not be staying with them before or after school."

"Did you call the sheriff 'cause you think your Daddy will hit you when you tell him?"

"No, I called the sheriff 'cause I know I won't kill my dad if the law is there. And I called Billy Harris 'cause he might shoot my daddy for me just 'cause he's a Watson."

That night Betty conducted herself with all the class and grace anyone could expect of any gentle, Southern Belle. She politely explained that James would not be coming over and they would not be needing their child care services any more.

Nadab started getting loud. "Get all uppity with me, little miss, and I will slap you around. Done it before, I'll do it again." And he took a step toward Betty.

At this point, Deputy Cooter Harris, who was leaning on his car, stepped up and in a really calm, deep voice said, "Mr. Watson, you raise a hand against Mrs. Worth and I will take you to jail by way of the hospital." The way he said it caused Nadab to realize he needed to be really careful what he did next.

So, he backed up a step and yelled out, "You can put on airs, but you are a Watson-white trash like the rest of us and you ain't never goin' to be no different."

"No, sir," Betty's voice was strong, but quivery, "I am a Worth and you will never take that from me or from my boy." And she walked away. Watson's always ended things with a fight or at least a cussing match. But Betty was clearly someone different.

On Monday morning before school, June Bug came into the kitchen and there was James. Seems that Caroline offered to watch after James before and after school 'til the end of the year. The three of 'em James, Beth Ann and June Bug would ride to and from school together and for several weeks had a grand time, but over Christmas break the Worth's moved to Montgomery. Doug got a route with Coke-a-Cola, so he was home every night and weekends and Betty was much closer to her work too. Betty never did go back to school, decided to stay home and have a family—two more boys and a girl. James did go to college and finally became a Doctor of Family Therapy. He was the first descendant of the Watson's to ever go to college. The Worth family didn't come back to McComb County much and when they did, they would only visit Betty's family for an hour or so and then they would leave.

But one time when James was back, he told June Bug, "You know that day my mama beat me was the last time she ever hit me. But she did beat the artist out of me. Haven't had the desire to draw since."

CHAPTER 4

Elias Black Shot the Pig out of the Tree

Some days are just too hot to do anything except sit in front of a fan and listen to stories. When it comes to listening to stories, the best place is a general store, the kind that Grandpa Lymon had. Being a storyteller himself, Grandpa Lymon tended to attract storytellers and the people who loved a good yarn. It was on one of the hottest days of the summer when June Bug first heard about the hog being shot out of the tree. The usual suspects were sitting on the porch of the store. Grandpa had a big pedestal fan set up so even if there wasn't any breeze it felt like there was one. Folks were drinking cokes out of bottles into which they had dropped roasted, salted peanuts and talking about wishing it was fall and how they couldn't wait till hog killing time. Hogs were generally butchered after it got good and cool, so that the meat would be less likely to spoil.

That is when Elias Black spoke up, "I once butchered a hog in the heat of summer, worst time of year, what with all the flies, and sweating hard, but can't wipe your face 'cause of all the blood on your hands."

"Why did you butcher in the summer, Mr. Black?" June Bug asked. Even June Bug knew you weren't supposed to butcher in the summer.

Mr. Black looked at June Bug and serious as a heart attack said, "Cause that is when I shot him out of the tree," he looked at Grandpa Lymon with what may have been a wink of his eye.

"Awe, come on, Mr. Black, hogs don't climb trees, you're funnin' me," June Bug said as he caught the nod between Mr. Black and Grandpa Lymon.

"No, I shot that hog out of the tree on July 6th, 1956. Butchered him up that day. Good thing we had a freezer, or we would have lost a lot of meat."

"Grandpa," June Bug says, "is Mr. Black teasing me?"

Grandpa simply said, "Let him tell the story and you can decide later."

That was all the encouragement Mr. Black needed. "I was clearing land to make room for row crops. I had been running hogs on this one spot-they are real good at rooting little things up. But when it comes to big stumps the best way to get them up is with dynamite. I had been blasting a few stumps out now and again and was getting close to being done. I was saving the biggest stumps for last because I was not knowing how much dynamite I would need. Well, I went down to the hardware store to pick up dynamite and they asked me if I was going to set it off for July 4th. That is how I remember when I blasted that stump. I got a half a box, so I had a good bit of the stuff.

"I was getting ready to get at this big, old stump and it was a big 'en. I figured I needed a lot of sticks to get it loose. I dug a hole down under it on one side as far as I could and I put the dynamite down in there with a long fuse. I lit the fuse and run over and lay down in a little ditch and looked up to see that the fuse was burning.

"What did I see? One of my hogs over there, snorting around and trying to figure out what was down in the hole. Well, I yelled at him, chunked some dirt clods and a pine stick at him, but he just ignored me. I seen the fuse was getting short so I lay down and covered by head. And "Kablouwee" the dynamite goes off; shook the ground I was laying on. When I looked up there is dust and smoke and the stump lay off to the side. But there ain't no hog." Here, Elias paused for the effect. "I go over to see if I can find anything left of it, but there ain't hide nor hair of that old boy. I start looking around to see him, but he ain't nowhere to be seen. Then I hear a grunt and when I look up there he is, stuck in the fork of a tree about 12 feet up. He is still alive, but his lower jaw is gone and he is lookin' real bad. So, I go over to the truck get my .22 and shoot him to put him out of his misery. Then I tied a loop on his leg and used the truck to pull him out of the tree."

There was a silence as Elias waited for June Bug's reaction. June Bug was wonder struck. He was, for one of the few times in his life, without words.

So Elias continued, "I am, as far as I know, the only man in the history of the state of Alabama to ever shoot a hog out of a tree."

The gathering on the porch laughed at that last line. They always did. Most of the men sitting there had heard the story before. The one man who didn't laugh was Brandon Watson. He was part of the Watson clan. Brandon wasn't one of the old retired men on the porch, or one of the school age boys on summer recess from school. Most men his age were at work this time of day, but Watson's avoided work if at all possible and were content to get a government relief check. Grandpa Lymon would occasionally extend credit to folks if they had a need. He let folks leave with groceries if they promised to pay in a day or two, but never a Watson. In one of his less charitable moments Grandpa Lymon was heard to say, "I wouldn't trust them to leave my store with air in their lungs if it weren't free."

Well, Brandon speaks up, "I may be doing a little summertime butchering. I seen a wild hog down at Beaver Dam Swamp that must weigh 400 pounds. I think I will go down there and shoot it; no use to wait till fall."

Nobody said anything for a moment then Grandpa Lymon said, "I guess I will believe it when I see it." Couple of folks chuckled, quiet-like, and Brandon got a little red in the face, but mostly there was a long drawn out silence. After a bit, a couple of older fellows said they needed to get home and started off. Elias said he needed coffee and joked that he could spend two hours at the store and have nothing to show but a pound of coffee. Grandpa Lymon got up to go in and take care of Elias' order and folks generally began to drift off.

When they were alone, June Bug asked Grandpa, "Did Mr. Black really shoot a pig out of the tree, Grandpa?"

"I expect so, son."

"You were kind of doubtful of Mr. Watson saying he saw a big hog in the swamp but you believe Mr. Black shot one out of a tree. Seems to me that Mr. Watson's story is more..." Here June Bug searched hard for the right words, "...like a true story, more believable."

Grandpa Lymon said, "'He that speaketh truth sheweth forth righteousness: but a false witness deceit'. Wise King Solomon wrote that about 3,000 years ago and it is as true now as it was then. I have known Elias Black for over 60 years and have found everything he says to be as true as the Good Book itself.

"Whereas with Brandon Watson, I have found that what serves him at the moment, be it truth or lie, is what he is going to say. The man who tells the truth is more believable in a far-fetched story than a liar is in a plain story. And the more a man lies, the more he wants to. Some of them Watson's would rather cross the road and climb a tree to tell a lie than to stand to your face and tell the truth. And if a man will lie about unimportant things, you can count on him being a liar if he thinks it will serve him."

"Is that why you won't give the Watson's credit?" June Bug asked.

"Yes, it is," Grandpa said, "Credit is a dangerous thing and I don't like to extend it, but sometimes it is needed. When a person buys on credit they're saying that they will pay it back. If they don't, it is wrong. Sometimes it can't be helped, but if they can pay and don't, they are liars. I know of some of them Watson's spending money on tomfoolery and letting their debts go bad. When that happens, I refuse them credit till they make it right."

June Bug got really serious and his face looked kind of sad. He looked up at Grandpa Lymon and asked, "Did mom tell you about the spit wad?"

"No, your mama didn't say anything about a spit wad."

"Would it be a lie if I said I didn't want to talk about it right now?"

"No, son, if your mama didn't feel the need to tell me, you don't need to tell me either, but if it's funny I think I want to hear about it."

CHAPTER 5

Mud Splashing: a Sport for Fools and June Bug was the Champ

Some sports will never make it big. According to the Mud Splashing League of Central Alabama, there were reasons why "Mud Splashing" would never be a big sport. Some of the boys said it was because there was no TV appeal. Some said it was because it was not for the faint of heart and most folks were just too chicken and some of the guys said it was because there was a bias against southern sports 'cause "Yankees" controlled the TV airwaves. But if the boys were honest, it would be because everyone who played kept it a secret, especially from their parents. It is hard for a sport to become popular if no one admitted to playing.

There were a lot of things these boys kept, or attempted to keep secret. But secrets are hard to keep, especially when you have friends who love to brag. For example, there was the time T.J. was bragging about how fast Robby drove across the river bridge. You see, T.J. and Robby were hanging out a couple of years after they had graduated from high school. They were both out on their own and they went over to see Robby's daddy and were talking about the good 'ole days (from three whole years ago) when T.J. opens his big mouth.

"Yea, Mr. Bakker, we was coming back from Montgomery one night and we knew the river was the county line and there wouldn't be no cops in that last couple 'o miles, so I tell Robby, 'Punch it, boy, punch it'. Well, he does and when we got to the top of that bridge we was going about 95 miles an hour. Man, that was a fast car."

Mr. Bakker, real calm-like, asked, "Was that my Pontiac that you're talking about?"

T.J. was thrilled to be talking; he usually was.

"Sure enough, Mr. Bakker, that was one bad car."

About this time, T.J. looked over to get confirmation from Robby who has been staring death at T.J. throughout the whole story, but T.J was too excited to notice. He sees Robby looking like he is going to kill him, when Mr. Bakker says, "T.J., Robby never told me that story, how fast do you think that car would go?"

T.J. realized he has messed up and started trying to take his words back. "Oh, I don't know, you know from where I was setting I couldn't see the speedometer very good, so we may have been going about 70 or even 60 that night, but I don't remember what we were doing that night. Isn't that the night we went to see that Burt Reynolds movie about the stunt driver?" Trying to change the subject, but not being too subtle about it.

The general consensus is that if Robby had not been living on his own his daddy would have thrown him out for driving like that. However, Robby and T.J. stayed friends. Robby explained, "T.J. is an idiot that talks too much. I knew that long before he told my dad about that trip back from Montgomery. And by the way, we were going 115."

There were lots of secrets to be known. Like skipping school to jump off the Tylor Goodwyn Bridge into the river, but getting Coach Trent to sign you in and out (this only worked for the basketball players). Or who was out parking at the old By Faith in Jesus Baptist Church off Bear Creek Swamp Road 10 miles out of town; everybody knew these folks weren't looking for Hootenannies. In a small community, there were lots of secrets to tell. One of the most closely held secrets was that of Mud Splashing.

No one knows how long the boys from south McComb County had been mud splashing. It tended to come and go a good bit. No one would splash for a long while, and then a couple of boys would take it up again. Or some of the younger boys would hear older brothers or uncles talk about it and they would take it up for a while. Some said that it began with the Hardy family way back when they settled this area after the Indians moved out.

To participate in Mud Splashing you never "played," you "participated" – it was too serious for play. All you needed was a .22 cal. rifle, a few cartridges and steady nerves. The two contestants would face each other about six feet apart, standing in mud. The best place to play was in Beaver Dam Swamp with all its flat, muddy places. The participants would shoot the mud in front of each other to try to splash mud on their opponent. The first person to flinch lost. Since a .22 isn't very loud, more often than not, the person would flinch when the mud hit them rather than the sound of the gun. The rule was you could shoot between your opponent's legs, but if the bullet hits the mud behind your opponent's heels you are disqualified and in danger of getting beaten to a pulp. Mud Splashing is a sport for fools.

June Bug was the champ of Mud Splashing. He never flinched no matter how much he got splashed. He would say, "I think of the war heroes like Uncle Sherman or Mr. Miller and I think about them fighting the Japs or the Commies and I think of that mud as if it was the blood of my enemies." June Bug could rattle on with his visions of glory.

Whether that is what he really thought or not it worked; June Bug almost never flinched. Dwight Thomas, who would later be called C.B., said, "You're just too stupid to flinch." Nathaniel

Jones would say, "Naw, he flinches. He's just so slow it won't happen 'til tomorrow." Nathaniel was the fastest of the boys and he was right, June Bug was pretty slow.

Sometimes after an afternoon of Mud Splashing, June Bug would have mud pretty near solid from his knees down and splashed here and there up to his shoulders. His mama would ask him how he got so muddy squirrel hunting, but June Bug just mumbled something about crawling about looking for a wounded squirrel. His daddy would say, "I'm glad we ain't counting on you to feed us. You can shoot up a box of shells and not get one piece of meat." They both knew the boys were playing more than hunting, but mama certainly had no idea what they were doing.

As the reigning champ, it was June Bug's privilege and duty to start the matches. There was a beginning ritual, which was passed down to these boys from a couple of older boys. Matches always began with the boys standing in a circle holding their hands out palms down-June Bug's hand was on the top 'cause he was the champ-and then yelling together "S.C"! That did not stand for South Carolina or Southern Cal, but for "spent cartridge". (They thought about calling themselves the "Spent Cartridges", but they decided that somehow lacked something) Then they would pair off and start splashing mud. When a boy flinched, his opponent won and moved on to the next match. The championship was usually June Bug against Harold Pratt or Dwight. Occasionally, June Bug lost, but that was pretty rare.

The last Mud Splashing was the crowning victory for June Bug. He won the last ever Mud Splashing event, so he will forever be the champ. Things had progressed as usual to the championship round. This time it was June Bug against Nathaniel Jones. As usual, June Bug was cool as a cucumber and looked like he was going to win. He shot about two feet in front of Nathaniel and the mud splashed up on Nathaniel and a little went as high as his face. Well, he closed his eyes and turned his head and the onlookers, who also served as referees, called "Flinch!" June Bug was a sure win now. Nathaniel would get one last shot because June Bug went first and if June Bug flinched, it would be a draw and they would have to re-match. June Bug never lost a draw.

Nathaniel fired and it sounded funny. June Bug gasped, but didn't move. Then after a moment, he let out a scream like he had been shot. Which he had. The bullet had hit a rock hidden in the mud and ricocheted off and creased June Bug's calf muscle.

It was pretty good cut and bleeding a good bit. June Bug started yelling and screaming and hopping on his good leg. Dwight starts fussing and carrying on, "Nathaniel, you shoot somebody; you're disqualified! If you're going to shoot people, you can't play." Nathaniel for his part was scared to death that his daddy would whip him with a briar. He yelled back at Dwight, "I didn't shoot him. I shot way in front of him!"

Dwight fires back, "He ain't bleeding for nothing; we all are going to jail now and it's your fault."

It was Harold Pratt that had a little common sense on this occasion, which was kind of odd 'cause usually Harold wasn't that bright. He took out a handkerchief and tied it around June Bug's calf. He told Dwight and Nathaniel to stop arguing and carry the guns back to Dwight's house. He was going to ride double with June Bug on his bicycle to Dr. King's office. The town was only a couple of miles away once they got up to the railroad track. Yes, it is hard to believe, but once upon a time boys not old enough to have a driver's license would go off to the woods with .22 rifles.

It only took about 15 minutes to get to Dr. King's office. On the way, June Bug talked about his life passing before his eyes like a big movie at the theater and Harold said it must have been a dull movie up to the end. When they got there, June Bug and Harold burst into the office and Harold said, "Somebody has been shot!"

The nurse looked up from the desk and said, "Who has been shot?" She thought they were talking about something on the radio, like when Kennedy was shot.

June Bug yelled, "Me! And I am going to die right here if you don't get Dr. King."

A lady in the waiting area said, "Nurse, he is bleeding" and pointed to blood-soaked pants.

When the nurse saw June Bug was in fact bleeding, she yelled, "Dr. King, Dr. King, come quick!"

June Bug thought Dr. King may have treated Civil War soldiers because he looked so old, but he was only a little older than DeRoy, June Bug's daddy. He grayed early and had a serious face. He was a big man and looked like he would have been a good prizefighter and had hands that were the size of a whole ham. He came down the hall, picked up June Bug and carried him to a room and put him on one of those tables that has paper on it. You know the kind that is like a roll of toilet paper, but real crinkly. He untied Harold's makeshift bandage, took hold of the pant leg and ripped it open to look at the wound. June Bug asked, "Dr. King, am I going to die?"

Dr. King grunted a little, looked at the muddy condition of Harold who followed them into the examination room and said, "You might when your mama finds out what you been doing. But you won't die from this little scratch."

"What I been doing?" June Bug thought to himself. He was about to protest that he was squirrel hunting when Dr. King said to the nurse, "Go call Caroline Johnson and tell her June Bug has got a scratch and I'm going to patch him up. She will need to come get him." The nurse left the room and Dr. King looked at Harold and said, "You want to watch?" Then to June Bug, "This is going to sting some."

To say it stung would be like saying a pole cat smells bad or Auburn dislikes Bama. June Bug claimed Dr. King scrubbed it with a brillo pad soaked in alcohol. Dr. King was actually very gentle both as a doctor and as a man.

June Bug's mama was out of the house the first time the nurse called, so by the time she answered the phone and got down to Dr. King's office, June Bug was sitting up and ready to go. When Dr. King heard the front door open and Caroline Johnson speak to the nurse, he looked at June Bug and said, "Act like you are about to cry."

Then his voice got really loud. "BOY, I SWEAR IF YOU ARE NOT CAREFUL I WILL CUT YOUR LEGS OFF AND SEE IF THAT WON'T LEARN YOU TO BE CAREFUL WHEN YOU GO HUNTING. ALL YOU BOYS ARE LUCKY I DON'T TURN YOU INTO THE STATE POLICE TO INVESTIGATE AN ACCIDENTAL SHOOTING."

About this time June Bug's mama came into the room. Dr. King turned to her and said politely and calmly as ever, "Mrs. Johnson, DeRoy is fine. He got a scratch while hunting today. Apparently, a bullet ricocheted off something and grazed his leg. I am certain it was an accident, but, later this week, I would like to talk with all the boys that were there. You can take him home now. I would suggest DeRoy take it easy for a couple of days. The nurse will tell you how to change the dressing on the wound." And with that he started out of the room. When he got to the door he turned around and said, "DeRoy, Harold," and holding his hand out, palm down, "S.C."

June Bug and Harold looked at each other, eyes wide and mouths dry, wondering how many other old people knew their secret. That Friday after office hours, as requested by Dr. King, all the boys were in the waiting area. Their parents thought it odd that Dr. King asked that the boys not be punished, but meet with him. The parents also found it odd that he asked them to wait outside 'til he was done. He sat down and said, "I mud splashed when I was your age. Some of your dads did, too. That may be why they ain't beat the tar out of you. When I was finishing my doctor's training, I was at Grady hospital in Atlanta; it's a big hospital. One afternoon I was working in the ER when they brought in this boy shot in the chest with a .22. The bullet clipped an artery near the heart. Every time the heart pumped, his blood filled up his chest. Me and a whole bunch of doctors. and nurses tried our best, but he died right there in front of us."

Dr. King's eyes filled up with tears and his voice got real crackly. "Worst thing ever happened in my life; watching that boy die. He and his friends were playing cops and robbers. One of the boys didn't have a toy gun, so he got a real one from somewhere. He unloaded it, or so he thought. While they were playing, he pointed it and pulled the trigger and killed a boy."

Dr. King picked up a Bible off of the table and opened it up. "In Proverbs 13:20 it says, 'He that walketh with wise men shall be wise: but a companion of fools shall be destroyed.' He closed the Bible, laid it down and looked around at the boys. "What that means is that if you keep company with people who are wise, you will learn from them. If you keep company with people who do stupid things, like mud splashing, you will end up hurt, dead, or stupid, which is almost as bad as being dead."

You would not have imagined that eight 11-to-13-year-old boys could be so still and quiet. Dr. King continued, "Instead of seeing who can come closest to shoot off someone's toe, why not see if you can help each other be wise. No more mud splashing and if I ever get wind of any of you boys or anybody else taking up that fool game, I swear I will tell your mama's and daddy's what you been up to. You hear me?" He waited for a moment then finished, "Now git."

The boys left and never a word was said by any of them about mud splashing. It was sort of known all around what happened and the rumors were better stories than the truth. Dr. King kept the secret too, but would remind the boys whenever they were in to see him for something. None of the boys became wise really quick, but they did stop doing stupid one thing at a time and that goes a long way toward being wise.

CHAPTER 6

You Can't Drown on a Sandbar

Smart and persuasive are not the same thing. There are some folks that don't have a lick of sense, but can somehow manage to get other folks to join them in their folly. There are some folks that have a little "horse sense," but if your horse sense ain't hitched up to a mulely stubbornness, it might get swept away like a stick floating on the current. That was what happened with June Bug. June Bug was a good boy and eventually he got his horse sense to grow a little mule-like stubbornness. It didn't happen all at once, but it started when folks thought he had drowned.

June Bug's parents were going to a Sunday school class picnic at one of the church member's river house and they took the kids along. June Bug didn't really want to go. He was afraid that he would end up having to take care of his little brother and sister Martin Lee and Katie Debra. As a concession to his protestations, his parents gave him permission to invite Dwight Thomas, which was somewhat of a consolation for June Bug. He figured that he and Dwight would manage to get into something and have some fun while the old folks had their party.

Sure enough, just as June Bug feared, before he and Dwight could run off to have some fun, Martin Lee wanted to go down to the water and Mama made it June Bug's job to watch out for him.

"June Bug," Caroline said trying to sound cheerful, "take Martin Lee down to let him look at the river. Now, see to it that he doesn't fall in or get muddy or get mud on his clothes."

"Yes, Mama," June Bug said being the very opposite of his mother's cheerfulness. He was pretty sure it was going to be as bad as he expected, but it was going to be worse.

With nothing to do but watch out for his brother, June Bug couldn't do much except walk around, hover over Martin to keep him and, therefore, himself out of trouble. As the three of them wandered along the riverbank they discovered an old, leaky boat tied up to the dock.

As they were standing there looking at the boat, Deroy, June Bug's dad, and Mr. Carter, the man who owned the river house, came up. "You boys want to take that boat for a ride, go ahead, if that's okay with your daddy," Mr. Carter said.

June Bug was thrilled when his dad said, "Yea, it will be okay. But ... " (and there always seemed to be a 'but') " ... don't take it out into the river. That current is pretty fast and it will carry you to Selma 'fore you know it and don't get out of eyesight of the dock." The river house was on a point where Black Turtle Creek empties into the Alabama River. Now, please understand that this creek wasn't much of a creek. It may have been 20 feet wide at the mouth, but up stream it wasn't much more than a boat length wide. It also meandered a lot, twisting and turning in the swampy lowlands where it drained. The restrictions meant the boys would not go far, do much, or be entertained for long.

But, it was better than walking around doing much of nothing; so, Martin Lee, Dwight, and June Bug got into the boat and using the one broken paddle started moving about the creek. Boredom set in pretty quick. They took turns splashing with the paddle and trying to find something to do. Martin Lee suggested they pretend to be Washington crossing the Delaware.

"What are we going to do once we get across?" June Bug said, kind of cross. "Why don't you pretend to be George Washington and invade the river house and leave us alone?"

"I don't have to. Anywhere you go, I can go," retorted Martin Lee. This was not turning out well. June Bug knew before long Martin would be having a hissy fit and they would all be stuck at the house with the old folks.

That is when Dwight came up with one of his great ideas. "Tell you what, why don't we go way up stream and you let me and Martin Lee out and we'll race you back to the dock?"

"We ain't supposed to get out of sight of the dock, remember?"

"Either that or we can sit here and do nothing 'til the sun melts our brains, or maybe go up to the house and watch a bunch of old people talk about how good life used to be when they were young. Besides it will be fun for Martin Lee." Dwight was hoping he would get Martin agitating for his plan. "It ain't gonna hurt nobody; we just get out and take off running. You'll turn around and start paddling back."

June Bug thought that was true-no harm would befall any of 'em. Fact is, Martin would be safer on land than in this old boat, which already had about 2 inches of water in it.

"Besides, we won't be out of sight for no more than a minute or two; nobody is going to notice."

Dwight turned to Martin and said, "I think your brother is just a little bit chicken. He is afraid you and me will beat him back to the dock." Martin Lee was now fully convinced that this was a thing they ought to do. There are some folks that are just persuasive; especially, if you want to be persuaded.

After thinking a while June Bug says, "Alright, if we do this, Martin, you have to promise you won't never tell nobody, ever, what we did. You tell and you won't never get to do anything fun again."

Martin agreed crossing his heart and exaggeratedly pretending to stick a needle in his eye.

Paddling hard against the current June Bug pulled up to a place on the creek bank that made it easy for Dwight and Martin to get out. Once they were out June Bug said, "Give me a shove and then you take off." Martin was about to push the boat when Dwight says, "Shove yourself, come on, Martin, let's go." And off they went.

June Bug yelled, "Cheater," but didn't waste time. He pushed really hard and tried to turn down stream. Here the creek was as narrow as the boat was long, so getting turned took some doing. June Bug knew there was no way he would get back first. He just wanted to get in eyesight of the dock before anybody noticed he was not where he was supposed to be. A couple of bends before he would see the dock June Bug was paddling hard, sweat just pouring off of him, when "it" happened. The creek had widened out a little and seemed to pick up speed getting really shallow. Because he was sitting way in the back of the boat with the bow riding high out of the water he did not notice the sand bar. This is also why the boat went so far up on the sand bar. It hit and threw June Bug off the seat and he caught himself on the middle bench. The boat stuck pretty firmly, especially with all the water that was in the boat.

About the time June Bug hit the sandbar, Dwight and Martin Lee reached the dock. Standing there was Deroy and Mr. Carter. "Boys, it is time to eat," Deroy said. Then continues, "Where is June Bug?" The boys looked at each other both knowing things had just gotten bad. Martin answered with a really weak, "I don't know."

"What do you mean, you don't know?"

Dwight pipes up, "He is supposed to be here."

Seeing the boys running up without June Bug, some of the folks up at the house started coming down to the dock. One of the first ones down was Dottie King. Miss Dottie was an old maid that loved a good crisis and if one wasn't on hand, she would go looking for one. She was known to go to funeral homes for the visitation of people she didn't know all that well just to see, "How folks was holdin' up." About the time Miss Dottie shows up Mr. Carter says, "I shouldn't have let them boys go out in that old, leaky boat." As far as Miss Dottie was concerned, it was time to start dragging the river for a body.

By now, most everyone was down around the dock, except Miss Dottie, who had gone to call the sheriff to send out a search team. Meanwhile, June Bug was standing on the sandbar trying to turn the boat over and get the water out. He heard his daddy calling his name and he answered right away.

Back on the dock everybody was talking, half of them admitted they had no idea what was going on, but they were willing to speculate anyway. The other half of the people were just getting warmed up for a good catastrophe. With all the noise, no one could hear June Bug answering back. To hear Dwight and Martin tell the story June Bug had paddled up stream almost to Birmingham, a good 120 miles away. One story led to another and within a few minutes the sheriff had a deputy on the way. The dispatcher radioed the message. The message was picked up by an airplane pilot who made a couple of passes over the river looking for a body. The low-flying airplane seemed to convince folks that the worst had truly happened. At the moment the airplane flew by, June Bug was standing ankle deep on water wondering why a pilot would be flying so low. At the dock, the only people who didn't seem to be terribly upset were Deroy, Caroline and the late arriving Grandpa Lymon. Knowing June Bug, they assumed he was in a mess but unhurt. Martin, for his part, was even crying 'cause he heard someone say June Bug was drowned.

June Bug eventually splashed out enough water to push the boat off of the sand bar. He climbed in and started paddling for the dock. He swore later that when people saw that he wasn't dead from drowning, they almost seemed disappointed.

When he got close to the dock, someone yelled out, "We thought the worst – thought you had drowned."

"You can't drown standing on a sand bar," he hollered back. Grandpa Lymon smiled, Caroline covered her mouth really quick, but his daddy said, "Watch your mouth and don't you sass your elders." As June Bug got out on the dock Mr. Carter said, "Nobody is hurt. Let's go eat."

June Bug walked up to his dad with Grandpa Lymon standing there and said, "I'm in trouble, ain't I?"

"Yep, you disobeyed me. Why did you do that?"

"Well, we were bored and Dwight got this idea of a race-them on foot, me in the boat. It didn't seem like a bad idea at the time." June Bug stood still and looked sadly at the ground.

"Aw, don't be too hard on the boy," Offers Grandpa Lymon. "Kind of reminds me of someone else that got carried away by bad council." He then smiled at June Bug, winked at Deroy and headed off to the house to eat.

Daddy stifled a smile for a moment, and then said, "Learn this lesson now. Don't take ideas from bone-headed people. Dwight is not an evil boy, just kinda foolish at times. I will tell you what your Grandpa told me once. I kept your mama out past her curfew time on a date one time. Some friends of ours had this great idea about a late movie. I knew we would be late getting home, but I figured we would be only a little late and it wouldn't matter much. When I got her home, Lymon was waiting for me. He can be a scary man." That was hard for June Bug to comprehend since Grandpa Lymon was always the picture of a sweet, easy-going, old man.

"After I explained what happened he looked at me and said, 'Go away from a foolish man, when thou perceivest not in him the lips of knowledge. If you are going to listen to your foolish friends you can stay away from my daughter.' I decided from then on I would only listen to wise people". Then after a long pause, June Bug's daddy said, "Well, we will deal with this later and you're not in big trouble, but for now, let's go eat."

CHAPTER 7

A Shooting at a Funeral

No story in all of the history of McComb County is sadder than the story of Sergeant and Mrs. Miller. Which means it has real potential to be funny in the end. When he was 18 years old, Olin Miller was informed by the Government that his neighbors thought it would be a good idea to go fight against the Nazis. Olin was not real happy about being "asked" to join the Army, so he ran off and joined the Marines. Turned out military life agreed with Olin. He was a natural leader and the Marines just made the most of it. He won a bunch of medals in the South Pacific, more than he ever let on about, and brought home a few stories to go along with the scars. One time during the war when he came home on leave, he asked his girlfriend, Gracie to marry him and when the war was over that is what she did. Sarge, that's what folks called him, stayed in the Marines for 25 years then came back home to settle in McComb County. Sarge and Gracie moved back home with their only child, a son Reuben Paul, who was 15 years old.

Reuben was sharp as a tack and a good boy. He graduated from high school and went to the University of Alabama to get a law degree. It also happened that while in Tuscaloosa he met and married a lovely little southern belle from down Mobile way, by the name of Sue Ellen Carter. After passing the bar Reuben and Sue Ellen moved to Montgomery where Reuben joined a law firm. They were living what seemed a charmed life. Rueben was having great success in the practice of law. He was universally popular with powerful, influential people in the state government. There was talk that he might start a run in politics. He was a great speaker, very handsome, well connected and charismatic.

But the most wonderful thing that happened was that a couple of years later, Reuben and Sue Ellen welcomed Sarge's first and only grandbaby into their home. Being less than 75 miles away, Sarge and Gracie got "Little Paul" every weekend. Little Paul adored his Nana and Pop and the grandparents seemed to live for the time they got with the boy.

When Little Paul would come out to McComb County he would spend a lot of time playing with June Bug. Living in a big city like Montgomery Little Paul didn't have the opportunity to play and get messy the way boys in the country did. So when he and June Bug got together he made the most of the opportunity to get dirty. It was hard to believe that two boys could get so covered with dirt, mud and who knows what else, or that they could smell so bad, so fast. Paul was all boy and full of energy. Sometimes after a rambunctious weekend of high-spirited and energetic play his grandparents were also glad to see him go home on Sunday night. Olin was heard to say, "If my Marines had carried as much energy as that boy we would have whipped the Japs in two months."

Now here is where the story gets terrible sad. One weekend while little Paul was with his grandparents, his mama and daddy were in a terrible car wreck. A drunk driver going about 100 miles an hour crossed the road and hit 'em head on. Reuben and Sue Ellen were killed instantly. They were tore up so bad that the funeral director had to have a closed coffin funeral. That made it really hard for the family. It was as if you couldn't say goodbye. Looking at those two, big, black boxes and knowing there was the body of a loved one inside ain't the same as looking on the cold still face and saying your last words to 'em. It makes grieving harder to do.

Reuben, being the lawyer he was, had his will set up so Paul came to be in the care of his Nana and Pop. The three of them was the saddest things you could have ever seen in your whole life. Before the accident all five of 'em were close and life was a joy, but now Olin, Gracie and Paul just barely hung on. Sarge had seen a lot of death in WWII and Korea but this was different. In war you expect to see people die, you know in some part of you that any day one of your friends might just buy the farm. But an accident is different. Last time you see them they are happy and whole, then they are gone. Sarge was strong on the outside, but everybody knew he was hurting real bad inside.

Gracie was the one everybody worried about. She seemed to be so fragile that a strong wind might just blow her to dust. She tried not to cry in front of people or even Paul or Sarge, but she was just so weakened by this all. This beautiful Southern belle seemed to wither to a shadow of what she once was. In one way she looked the same as ever, but it was like looking at a drawing, you know it is only a representation of what used to be there.

And Little Paul? Well, he just started acting up. He was a good boy and had never gotten into the least trouble before hand, but after his parents died he was always getting into trouble. Moving to a new school is hard, but in these conditions it was especially hard. Little Paul would see people look at him and then whisper and he would go punch 'em. The teachers and principle were understanding and tried to help as they could but Little Paul was getting hard to control. He even started fighting with his best friend on earth, June Bug. June Bug tried to keep being friends with Paul, but it usually ended up with Paul saying nasty things to June Bug or the two of 'em getting into a real fight not just fun rough housing. Got so that June Bug stopped asking to go over to see Paul and never asked him to come over.

June Bug asked his mama, "Why do folks let Paul act like he does? If I did half the stuff he did I would be slap wore out." His mama tried to explain, but it didn't make sense to June Bug. Well, the sad thing is things got worse.

Sarge had a heart attack and it was a bad one. Old Dr. King came as fast as he could, but it was no use; Olin was dead before Dr. King got there. Most folks believed that Olin died the night he heard the news about Reuben, but his heart was so strong it kept running for a few months anyway. Miss Gracie was all done in. She had suffered more loss in less than a year than the rest of her life put together. Now she had a rowdy little boy that needed a strong hand from a man to keep him in line and she was just barely able to get up in the mornings, let alone have the strength to manage a strong-willed, rebellious boy.

It was a terribly, sad situation.

The funeral for Olin was held in the high school gym on account no church would have been big enough. Because Olin was a war hero, the Marines sent a color guard and military chaplain to show respects. As it turns out no one knew half the heroic things that Olin had done during the war. A Marine Major got up and read a list of awards and service medals and actions Sarge had won or been a part of. People always respected Sarge, but this changed things and took it to a higher level.

Well, after the service they loaded the coffin in the hearse and they started the procession to the graveyard. All during the service everyone sat stock-still and listened except little Paul. He was acting out something awful. June Bug was a wondering when someone was going to pop Paul upside the head, but no one ever did.

On the way to the cemetery, June Bug asked Grandpa Lymon, "Grandpa, why don't somebody straighten out Little Paul? He ought not act the way he does."

Grandpa Lymon sighed really deep. He was grieving 'cause he had known Olin since they were boys. "The Good Book says,

'The heart knoweth his own bitterness; and a stranger doth not intermeddle with his joy.'" Then he just looked out the car window as they rode along.

"What does that mean, Grandpa?"

"Well, it means that no one can know how deep a person is hurting and sometimes when people are hurting real bad they can do strange things. Your uncle Sherman was as finer man as ever lived, but he come back from his war hurting real bad and took to drinking. Nobody says it is right, but hurting people let it out in strange ways.

"Deroy," (Grandpa almost never called him Deroy unless it was real serious), "Little Paul has lost more than any of us could know. It may be like dying inside, so everybody is a little extra patient. He needs you and all the people who care about him to keep loving him." June Bug felt a little ashamed of feeling ill toward little Paul, but for the moment he just sat real quiet.

Now, here is where it gets real funny. At the graveside, Little Paul was sitting next to Miss Gracie and he was still cutting up and carrying on. Miss Gracie was trying to keep him under control but not having much luck. The preacher said a few words and the chaplain said a few words. The soldiers folded up Old Glory and handed it to Miss Gracie. It was real peaceful, until the first round of the 21- gun salute was fired. I'm not sure if Miss Gracie knew they were going to have a 21-gun salute or not, but if she did, it must have slipped her mind. At that moment, she was down to her last good nerve, what with the loss of her son, daughter-in-law, husband and having to take care of little Paul. As soon as that first report sounded, Miss Gracie fainted dead away. She fell slap out of her chair right there on the ground. Little Paul jumped at the sound and when he saw his grandma fall over he leaped out of the chair and yelled at the top of his lungs, "Somebody call the cops! Those sons of b****** just shot Nana!"

Folks didn't know what to do. More than a few started laughing including the preacher and the chaplain; out of respect they all tried to hold it in. Several people gasped and looked in horror and a couple of people were visibly angry. June Bug just started walking up to little Paul-couldn't say why he did-Grandpa Lymon right behind him. When he got to him, Paul looked at June Bug and it wasn't the face of someone trying to be funny or mean or putting on, it was somebody scared.

June Bug said, "Paul, it will be okay." And then the strangest thing happened. Little Paul ran up to June Bug and Grandpa Lymon and hugged Grandpa Lymon and commenced to crying the hardest cry ever was. The first time he had cried really hard since his mama and daddy died. He hugged Grandpa Lymon for the longest time and just cried.

The women folk revived Miss Gracie and got her up in her chair. Little Paul let go of Grandpa Lymon and sat by his grandma and they cried together for a while. Eventually, everybody left to go to the dinner brought in by the church folks. One thing about a little southern town, they take care of widows and orphans-neither Miss Gracie nor little Paul ever wanted for anything. I wish I could tell you Little Paul never acted up again, but that would not be entirely true. It would be true to say that June Bug and Grandpa Lymon became a big part of little Paul's life and he grew up to be a fine young man. He lived with Miss Gracie 'til he went away to seminary to study to become a preacher. Miss Gracie didn't live to see him graduate, but she did live long enough to hear him preach a few times. Little Paul never came back to McComb County, but every time there is a military funeral and they have a 21-gun salute, the people of McComb County think about Little Paul.

CHAPTER 8

Grandpa Lymon Loves "Precious Memories"

A fifth Sunday Sing happens on the fifth Sunday of the month when churches dismiss regular evening services and get together and spend the evening singing. And you would not believe what someone said at one of the singings. It was a word that lasted only a moment all those years ago, but what happened afterwards is remembered in McComb County at every fifth Sunday sing to this day. Fifth Sunday singings were a big deal in McComb County. They were not scheduled weeks in advance, but rather years in advance. Folks planned for a fifth Sunday singing with much excitement and anticipation like it was the second coming of the Lord Himself. This was especially true when the fifth Sunday singing was at June Bug's church. Every church that hosted a fifth Sunday singing did something special and tried to outdo all other churches (for the glory of God, of course). If your church hosted a fifth Sunday sing and it was kind of poor, you would not get the opportunity again for a long time.

Several churches got one pretty near every year. First Baptist usually got a summer month and would host a watermelon cutting. They would have watermelons stacked all over the yard and after the singing was over everybody would go outside, eat watermelon and visit. Kids would chase fireflies, play tag, hide-n-seek, "haint in the bushes" and generally run themselves ragged. Teenagers would flirt, court, and try to act innocent while the adults would sit in lawn chairs and talk until full dark. Wesley Chapel United Methodist would work with Great Pisgah AME church for a fall, fifth Sunday Barbeque. They generally held it at the park near the high school and would accept donations for the football team-five dollars a plate or twenty dollars a family. At these you could count on the white trash Watson's bringing every member of their clan and claiming it was just one family. When Cooter Harris got on the board at Wesley UMC that stopped, sure enough. Sometimes the singing would be all Christmas songs if the fifth Sunday was in November. That was always a good one. After several congregational carols, each church choir would do one special and then off to a feast of Christmas desserts and candy canes for the kids.

But of all the fifth Sunday singings there was no hog at the trough bigger than June Bug's church. The Cambridge Community Church was out in the country a bit and made up of mostly farming families and one thing is for sure, farm women know how to cook. Now the Cambridge Church made its name by two things. First, was the fellowship after the singing. At Cambridge, you could only bring pie and maybe ice cream. The women, for the glory of God of course, worked for weeks to outdo each other in making pies. You would have a hard time naming a pie that was not brought by the women of Cambridge.

Were I able to describe the taste of those pies, you would drop what you are doing right now and go searching for some pie. And when you found it you would be disappointed because compared to the pies of Cambridge, the pie you found would seem dry and tasteless. The fellowship hall at Cambridge was right next to the sanctuary. Miss Lizzy, who was about 300 years old, insisted on cooking her pies at church, so that they would be piping hot.

So, about 40 minutes into the singing, the smell of baking pies would begin filling the sanctuary and signal it was time to end the singing.

The other thing that made Cambridge singings special was the music. They never had soloist or specials; all the singing was from the congregation. If you wanted to request a special song you stood in line and when it was your turn you would lead the congregation in singing. More than a few young people got themselves on stage for the first time this way. After a while the church choir director Rodney White, music teacher at the school, would conduct class. He would have an easy song picked out and would teach parts. His wife played the low notes and he would have all the men sing this, then high voiced women sing that, then the low voiced women sing another part. After all this, he would say, "We are going to do a concert of this song for God. He is listening to hear His children sing, so do a good job." Then the whole church would sing like a choir and it was always real good. The last part of the singing was always the "Sing Song".

The way a "sing song" worked was someone on the right side of the church would yell out a word, any word. The first person to stand up on the left side of the church named the hymn that word brought to mind and then the congregation would sing that song. They would switch back and forth for a few songs to wind up the evening's singing. Sometimes the songs would come to mind really easy. Someone would yell out, "Cross," and somebody from the other side would stand up and say "The Old Rugged Cross." But sometimes it was harder to think of a song; some folks spent a good deal of time thinking of words that might stump the congregation.

On one occasion, the church was packed full of worshipers and the smell of Miss Lizzy's pie was creeping in and it was about time to dismiss and go eat pie. June Bug was sitting on the second row with Grandpa Lymon this Sunday night. He usually sat with Grandpa Lymon, but sometimes he would set with all the other teenage boys on the back row. On this occasion, he was very thankful he was sitting next to his grandpa. Mr. White had done about four songs and said, "We will do one more sing song and then be dismissed, so somebody from the right side give me a word."

From the back benches one of the teenage boys yelled out, "Sex!"

A silence fell over the church that was like the sound of a funeral home at midnight. A pin drop would have sounded like thunder. Mr. White's mouth dropped open, Mrs. White who was the more hot-tempered of the two sat on the piano bench and her face was as red as the filling in Miss Lizzy's cherry pie. Mrs. Horn who played the organ was the color of a bed sheet except for her blueish hair. No one was sure who yelled out "sex," in church, but every boy on the back row knew he was in for it. Being in the general proximity of such a sin was enough to bring, if not the wrath of God, at least the wrath of parents. Even the preachers were shocked into stock stillness.

It may have been only two or three seconds, but it seemed like maybe an hour when Grandpa Lymon stood up. He turned toward the back row and looked over the boys now cowering in their seats. Everyone in the house expected a verbal chastisement from the oldest, godliest man in the county. Everyone there knew, loved, and respected Grandpa Lymon. If he had said, "Take every boy out and whip 'em all," it probably would have happened. Every eye was on this grand saint, every ear straining to hear what he would say. Grandpa Lymon turned and looked at Mr. White. In a voice that was feeble and coarse he said two words, "Precious Memories."

No one grasped what he had said, not even Mr. White. He looked blankly at Grandpa Lymon and said, "Pardon, Mr. Baker, what did you say?"

In a voice that quavered and may have been a bit of a put-on Grandpa Lymon said, "That boy said, 'Sex,' and that brings to mind 'Precious Memories'."

It took a moment for the impact of that statement to sink in. Then a flooding tide of laughter swept the tension from the room. Everyone laughed. Even those who would later swear they didn't laugh were laughing. Pastor Mann laughed 'til he cried. Mrs. Horn couldn't play the organ she was laughing so hard and Mr. White, once he got the song going, just stood there and waved his arms in time to the music. The congregation finished the song with the words of that great old hymn, which forever after held new meaning, "In the stillness, of the midnight precious, sacred scenes unfold."

After the song ended, Rodney White prayed a blessing, dismissed the crowd and everyone went happily to pie.

June Bug sat with Grandpa Lymon until the church house was empty. Other people would stand in line for Grandpa Lymon, so he need not hurry to find a seat or get in line and he was content to smile and wait for the crowd to thin down a bit.

"Grandpa," June Bug began, "why did you do that? I was expecting Mr. White or Preacher Mann to say something real stern to them boys. But you turned it into a joke. Why?"

"June Bug, the Good Book says: 'All the days of the afflicted are evil: but he that is of a merry heart hath a continual feast.' Them boys was just wanting to show-out and make a stir. I am pretty sure that their mamas and daddies will deal with their folly at home. But there wasn't any cause to allow one foolish child to cast a bad cloud over our pie eating."

"What they did was wrong?"

"It was, not 'cause sex is wrong nor because trying to be funny is wrong, but because they wanted to hurt people, to shock people. But I figured the best thing anyone could do was laugh at them and laugh at ourselves a little." After a long pause Grandpa said. "June Bug, how about we go fill up on pie and ruin our supper?"

Turns out it was Jerry Thomas who was the one who yelled out – did it on a dare from a couple of other boys. They all took a good whipping and out of the goodness of their daddies' hearts they cut the yards of First Baptist, Wesley Chapel, and Cambridge all summer long. For free no less.

Several years later when Grandpa Lymon died, at his request for his funeral the church choir sang "Precious Memories" and there wasn't a dry eye in the house. But it seemed that a lot of folks were crying 'cause they laughed so hard.

CHAPTER 9

Cussing in Church

G randpa Lymon was well known in McComb County for helping out any church that needed help. He was a member at the Cambridge Church and had at different times served on the board, taught Sunday School, and even did an occasional turn in the nursery. But when he was able he also helped out other churches around. On one occasion, he stood up for cussing in the church house.

The Crooked Creek Church was looking for a preacher. They asked Lymon if he would consider being their minister, but he declined. But he did offer to help them look for a preacher and while they were looking he would attend there to try to encourage the folks a little. Grandpa Lymon took June Bug as a companion on these Sunday trips. It was on account of this that June Bug heard the cussing in the church house.

The preacher that Sunday was Randy Kent. Randy wasn't brought up in anything like a Christian home. It might not be far from the truth to speculate that his first words were cuss words. Growing up with a mama and daddy that would have a cuss fight he learned the words real early. When Randy graduated from high school he joined the Marine Corp. In the Marines he learned a new intensity to his profanity. It was as if his goal in life was to replace the saying, "Cuss like a sailor" with "Cuss like a Marine".

You might say that cussing was his native language. On one occasion an old Marine sergeant said, "Boy, I think you got a cussing problem." When a Marine sergeant thinks you may cuss too much, you cuss a lot.

Randy didn't cuss just when he was angry. He had a cuss for every occasion, good or bad. If he were happy, he would cuss. If he were sad, he would cuss. He especially cussed when he would get excited. If he got worked up over something, 'most every word he said would be a cuss word.

But the strangest thing happened to Randy. Through circumstances that only God could arrange he became a Christian. Not one of those "Sunday only" kind of Christians, but the real McCoy. Randy was a changed man and there was no doubt about it. It seemed that all the vices of his life let go pretty easy, except for cussing. He battled and resisted cussing, but it was no easy task. That was because he started cussing long before he started drinking, chasing women, or smoking. Being in the Marine Corp is not an easy place to quit the cussing habit. While in the Corp, Randy sensed that he was receiving the call to become a minister, so when his hitch was up he left the Marines and went to Bible college.

It was during Randy's first year in college that Grandpa Lymon called someone he knew at the college and asked the college to send a student down for a trial sermon. The way a trial sermon worked is a prospective preacher would come down on a Sunday morning and would preach his best sermon. Afterwards, he would have an interview where he would tell the church leaders what a good preacher he was. The church leaders would tell the prospective preacher what a wonderful church they were. Both sides were known to exaggerate just a bit. Generally, they would have a fellowship meal and afterwards the congregation would talk about the preacher, take a vote and if he got enough votes he would become the new preacher (if he wanted to their preacher).

Crooked Creek wanted a young man that would be willing to come every weekend, preach, teach a class and do an occasional funeral. The college recommended Randy because of him being a little older than most of the students-he seemed more mature. Randy was as nervous as a long-tail cat in a room full of rocking chairs about the whole prospect. But with lots of help from friends and teachers, he was able to put together a sermon and was as well prepared for the interview as he could be. He was a natural speaker and had a commanding presence when he talked to people. He was also quite handsome and still had the bearing of a Marine.

Randy arrived at the church and found himself very excited to preach his first sermon. He had decided to preach on the temptation and fall of Adam and Eve (mostly because that was what they had talked about in one of his classes that week). After the singing and offering and an introduction by Grandpa Lymon, Randy got up to preach. His voice boomed in the old church house and the congregation sat in rapt attention. Randy talked first about how good the apple looked. Then he talked about how foolish Adam and Eve were to even listen to temptation. He was doing a great job for a fellow who had never preached before. As Randy preached he gathered steam and every now and then he would hit the pulpit with a fist. He was huffing and sweating and really pouring it on. It was just the kind of preaching that the old, country folk loved.

His final point was on what an evil character Satan is. He talked about how he could never be trusted, being a liar. "Satan is the enemy of your soul and has no intention for you but harm." He thundered. By this point Randy was getting away from himself a little. His words were coming faster than his brain could manage them.

"I will tell you that dirty, double-crossing scoundrel is the sorriest, no-count, son-of-a-b@*#& that ever lived! If you give him half a chance he will f*#@ you over and...."

At this point, Randy realized what he had done. He had slipped back into his old Marine words. He stopped mid-sentence and looked over the congregation. They sat there eyes wide and mouths hanging open, it didn't seem like there was even one of them breathing. Grandpa Lymon and June Bug sat on the second pew. Grandpa Lymon had his brow so knitted together it looked like a once-plowed field. June Bug looked afraid ... really frightened ... as if he expected the roof to be split open by fire from on high at any moment. There is never a silence like the silence in a church after someone slips up and cusses and Randy did a dandy job of cussing.

Randy almost broke down in tears. He was so ashamed that he couldn't even word an apology. He saw the shock on the faces of the little congregation and simply stepped out of the pulpit and went and sat down on the front bench. He didn't look like a proud Marine or even a young preacher. He looked like a dog that had been beat all its life. He looked like he might just curl up on the front pew and cover his face with a hymnbook. He just slouched there hoping everyone would just leave without him having to talk to anyone. In that moment, he decided he would go back to school, drop out of college, and go back into the service.

That is when, Grandpa Lymon stood up and took just three steps to stand next to Randy and turned to face the congregation. He put one hand on Randy's shoulder and extended the other to the congregation, hand up as if asking for a coin. After a moment that seemed like a year to Randy, Grandpa Lymon spoke.

"I don't care much for the way he said it, but I sure am glad to know which side he is on. I think this church ought to hire this young man. I think he could do with a bit more training, but you got to admire how he feels about the enemy." He then dismissed the church with a prayer and the women folks went off to fix the fellowship dinner.

Not everyone was eager to have a cussing preacher, but it was decided that if he wouldn't cuss they would be proud to have him come down on Sundays to preach. The good folks of the Crooked Creek Church did come up to Randy and tell him not to worry too much about a little slip up. One older farmer came up and said, "H*** son, I was a Marine back in World War II. I think we might be able to understand each other." That is how Randy 'Ole Cuss' Kent became the preacher at the Crooked Creek Church.

That day on the ride home from church June Bug asked his grandpa, "Do you really think that preacher will be a good one? I mean he let loose a couple of really bad words in the church house besides." June Bug was genuinely confused about his grandpa speaking up for a cussing preacher.

"'Faithful are the wounds of a friend; but the kisses of an enemy are deceitful.' The Book of Proverbs says that. What it means is that the truth we don't want to hear is better than the flattery we like to hear. Randy was telling what he really felt deep down in his heart when he said those cuss words. It would have been better if he had said it without cussing. But I would rather have true conviction come out, than false words that might make me feel better." After a little pause he added, "I think he will make a fine preacher someday."

It turned out Grandpa Lymon was right (he usually was about these sorts of things). It was a good match for both Randy and the Crooked Creek Church. He stayed there the whole time he was in Bible College and a few years besides. The church grew to be a pretty good-sized church for a rural congregation. And when he moved on to another ministry, he left as a good friend to the people and with a lot of memories, most of them good ones.

It would be nice to say that Randy never cussed again. It would be nice, but it would not be entirely square with the truth. It would be true to say he never cussed in the pulpit again. There were occasions when he would get riled up in a sermon and then would have a long silence. Folks assumed that he was censoring himself and looking for a non-cuss word to use instead. Over the years, it got easier for Randy to not cuss. He did say, "When someone does or says something really stupid those old Marine words pop right to the front of my mind and sometimes it is hard to hold 'em back. I don't cuss anymore, but if someone else will, I'll say, 'AMEN'!"

CHAPTER 10

Living Dead Man

ny way you sliced it old Mr. Marsh was weird. You could put any label on it you want. Some people said he was eccentric, some said he was creepy, some said he was crazy, and others thought things that were much worse, but there was no getting around it: he was one strange duck.

First of all, he was almost never seen, didn't come to town very often, didn't attend any of the churches, and never visited anyone. Second, he always wore black: black pants and a black shirt. Occasionally, he would wear a white shirt, but only when he had on a black coat. If he ever wore anything different no one knew about it. His house was scary too. It was between town and Grandpa Lymon's place out the highway apiece. The house sat by the road surrounded on three sides by a big cotton field. Mr. Marsh owned the land, but he didn't farm anymore; he just leased that land to other folks. The house was a real big, two-story house, the kind that has big, majestic columns from the porch to the roof. Once up on a time it must have been grand, but it was run down now. The bushes were grown up tall and the tree limbs crowded in on it. It looked like it needed to be haunted if it wasn't already. But what was the worst thing about the Marsh place was the stuff Mr. Marsh put out in the yard.

The yard was full of weird things. It was full of old air conditioners, fans, refrigerators and crosses. On every one of these Mr. Marsh had written things like: "Hell is hot," "There ain't no cool water in hell," and "There is not an air conditioner in hell." There must have been 150 different things all with some message on them about it being hot in hell. It seemed that every broken air conditioner, fan, refrigerator or freezer in all lower Alabama was sent to Mr. Marsh to be given a painted message and consigned a place in the yard for all eternity. Some folks joked about Marsh's place being "appliance hell" for wicked appliances. It is not hard to understand why there were so many rumors about Mr. Marsh.

One late afternoon in October, June Bug and Grandpa Lymon were riding along in grandpa's truck and happened to see Mr. Marsh coming out of the hardware store carrying a couple cans of paint. Grandpa Lymon glanced over and said, "Looks like ol' Harry got another air conditioner box to paint."

June Bug, who was in a feisty mood piped up, "I wish somebody would burn that old man out. Set fire to that old house and burn it to the ground. Then they ought to take a bulldozer and dig a big old hole and push all that junk in and cover it over."

"Hush up, boy, don't you talk like that. You got no business saying such a thing. Harry Marsh never did you, or anybody else, any harm."

"But, Grandpa, I heard all kinds of things about him. They say he is a devil worshiper. That he has killed a bunch of people and he keeps his family chained up in the basement of the house, and he preaches to 'em about hell every night." June Bug got all excited as he talked.

"'They say,' 'they say.' You can always tell somebody is repeating a big lie when they start off with, 'They say'. June Bug," and here Grandpa's voice got noticeably softer, "them stories you have been hearing and telling are pure and contemptible lies. Not a soul that has repeated them knows the first thing about Mr. Marsh. If they did, they wouldn't tell lies about him."

"Do you know him, Grandpa?"

"Yep, most of my life. He is a little younger than me, but we were in school together. His family has owned that farm for the last 100 years, but he is the last of the Marshes."

"He don't keep his sons and daughters chained up in the basement?"

"He never had any daughters and his only son died before you were born."

"What happened, Grandpa?" June Bug had visions of some terrible story of murder or some such.

"Jasper Marsh was a little younger than your mama. He was the only child of Harry and Karen. Harry learned from his daddy how to be a good farmer, how to work the land and how to be good at business. That farm was the picture of productivity. When the cotton was ripe it would look like a blanket of snow covered the land in all directions from their home. They were doing mighty well. Harry was teaching Jasper all about running the farm. Took him with him anytime he could, let him have a say in hiring help and even took him to meetings with the banker. Harry was hoping Jasper would keep the family farm running.

"Well, one Christmas they went on a vacation. Went up to New England to see real snow and went to New York City and had a big vacation. But Jasper come down with something, thought it was a cold, but it settled in his lungs. He was dead within a month. Poor ol' Karen grieved herself to death. She took to a sick bed and never got up. There was no disease or sickness except a broken heart. Harry lost his only child and his wife in a matter of months. He suffered the loss of his present and his future all at one time."

"Is that why he is the way he is?"

"If you mean 'sad', yes. For a while, after he buried Karen, he acted like everything was going to be okay. But finally he stopped pretending and just gave into the grief. He stopped caring about the farm and eventually just leased it all to someone over in Autauga County. Once he did that, he had a lot of time on his hands and not enough to do."

"Were you his friend when all this happened?" June Bug was genuinely saddened by the story.

"I'm still his friend. But, yes, we were pretty close back then. We went to church together and had some business doings together. I went to see him every week from when Jasper died till about two years after Karen died."

"Why did you stop?" June Bug's little mind was trying to wrap around this story and he wanted every detail.

"He said he needed to be left alone. So, I stopped going out so much. I cut back to once a month and then to about once every six months. Now, I just go out every now and again, but Harry don't talk much. He just wants to be left alone to..." Grandpa Lymon thought real hard what to say next. "...To carry out his ministry."

"His ministry? What ministry? Does he have someone that he preaches to about hell?" June Bug could not conceive of anything other than preaching as being a ministry.

"No, he sometimes calls his warnings about hell painted on old appliances as his ministry."

They rode along for a while neither of them saying anything. After what was a record long silence for June Bug he finally broke the silence. "Grandpa, did Jasper go to hell?'

Then realizing the awkwardness of the question, he added, "I mean with all the signs and messages about hell and all I was wondering if Jasper was a wicked sinner condemned to hell?"

Grandpa Lymon was quiet for a while and June Bug began to think he might have said something really terrible.

"Son, only the Lord can judge if a man goes to Heaven or Hell. We may have a guess, but that is God's right to judge not ours. But Harry is terrified that he did. The Marshes were church people, but not very faithful. And going to church makes you a Christian about like going into a garage makes you a Ford. About the time that Harry asked to be left alone, he had a nightmare that kept coming back. He dreamed that Jasper was in Hell asking for a drink of cold water. It must have been a terrible vivid dream for Harry, 'cause he was never the same afterwards. He was afraid that his boy was in Hell because he had failed to do right by his religious upbringing."

Grandpa drove along quietly, his mind racing over the years. "You see, all them signs Harry puts up is to keep someone else from suffering. He has spent most of his money and time trying to tell people that they don't want to go to Hell. I believe Harry really cares about people, but his grief has confused the way he sees things."

"Grandpa, is Mr. Marsh crazy?"

"Not in any way that would make him a danger to anyone, but I am afraid that his grief and the fear left by that nightmare may have messed up his mind."

It was just before sunset when they passed the old Marsh place surrounded by hundreds of warnings about the horrors of Hell. The place was especially scarier in the twilight. The lights in the review mirror of the truck meant that Mr. Marsh was not far behind. He would go out to the barn to an old refrigerator or air conditioner and spend his lonely evening painting a message that he desperately hoped would turn someone from perdition.

"Grandpa," June Bug's voice was barely audible above the noise of the road, "That may be the saddest story I have ever heard."

"Yes, son, it is. As the wise old king Solomon said, 'Even in laughter the heart is sorrowful and the end of mirth is heaviness.'"

"What does that mean, Grandpa?"

"Well, I suppose it means that in every life there will be sorrow. Even if we try to hide it, sometimes the sorrow is just too big to hide. That is why the Lord wants us to love everybody, 'cause deep down everybody has a hurt."

CHAPTER 11

Bust 'em in the Mouth

You could have knocked June Bug over with a feather. He stood there slack-jawed and speechless and he was never speechless unless he was talking with a pretty girl.

"Close your mouth, Son, a bug may fly in," said June Bug's grandpa.

"Grandpa, did you just say I may have to bust Randall Hardy in the mouth? I ain't never heard you talk about fighting someone."

"I don't generally advocate fighting, but sometimes it is the only option and if that is the case, then it needs to be done," said Grandpa.

What started it all was something that happened at school that morning. Terrance Jones was a good friend of June Bug's who just happened to be black. The races got along better in McComb County than in most small Southern towns. Generally, it was because Grandpa Lymon and Pastor Horace Jones lead their communities to respect each other. But in every society there had to be some fool who liked to stir stuff up. One of those characters in McComb County was Randall Hardy.

Terrance was a second cousin of Pastor Horace, a very good student and a fine young man. It looked like he might be the first black valedictorian in Robert Frost High School's history. Randall, on the other hand, was about, but not quite, as bright as a bucket of bricks and he hated the fact that Terrance always bested him in every subject.

The Hardy's were almost all racists and the ones that weren't on the outside probably were on the inside. It galled Randall to no end to have one of his teachers tell him he was going to fail math and that maybe he could ask Terrance to tutor him and help him get his grades up to passing. Maybe the teacher was trying to shame Randall into working harder or maybe she just wasn't thinking about it, but, for whatever reason, she put Terrance in a bad spot.

That day after lunch, Terrance and June Bug were walking down the back hall to 5th period biology. June Bug was having trouble and was hoping Terrance could help him. Randall stepped out in front of Terrance and blocked his way. He puffed out his chest and said, "Hey, boy, this hallway is off limits for you from now on. You got to go around the other way to go to class. If you come this way tomorrow I will put a hurting on you."

Randall was a lot bigger than Terrance. He had been in more than a few fights and had been suspended several times. Terrance, on the other hand, came from a family that was real peaceable. Terrance had most likely never so much as thrown a punch in anger. So this looked real bad for Terrance. All of a sudden, everyone realized it was deathly quiet in the hall.

June Bug spoke up, "Come on, Terrance, let's go."

Later that afternoon when June Bug told Grandpa Lymon what happened, Grandpa simply said, "Sounds like you may have to bust Randall in the mouth with all your might."

June Bug closed his mouth, but only for a moment, "Grandpa, I ain't never heard you speak about fighting. I mean not like that. Why?" June Bug was having a hard time getting words to come out. He felt for a moment like he was talking to a complete stranger.

"Let me tell you what my daddy said to me one time. But to understand what he said, you need to hear a story." There were few occasions in life that didn't remind Grandpa Lymon of a story.

"When I was 12 years old we had a very wet, rainy winter; wettest one I can remember. It was so wet that year that the road by our farm washed out and folks who lived out towards Laurel Crossroads couldn't get their wagons or buggies into town. Even horses had a hard time getting by. Daddy cut down the fence by the field so folks could get off the road for a piece, go through the field and get around the wash out. He did it just to make it easier for folks to give them a way to get back to where the road was good.

"A couple of weeks before it was time to start planting, daddy took us boys to fill in the washed-out road and fix the fence. I was 12, my brother Leon was 14, and my oldest brother, Lynard, was 15. We were still boys, but daddy made sure we carried man-size responsibility and could do man-size work. He also let us each carry a pistol. There were a lot of rattlesnakes out that way back then, so it was pretty common for us to carry a pistol in our pockets most of the time.

"One day, Leon and I were coming in from the garden and we come up on this rattlesnake about four feet long. It was making for the hen house. Leon took his pistol out and shot it from about 10 to 12 feet. Hit that snake about two inches behind the head and blew his head clean off. I could never shoot as good as Leon, but I was about as good as Lynard. Anyway, back to the story...." (Grandpa Lymon had a tendency to get side-tracked on other stories).

"Before daddy would start fixing the fence he had us fill in the wash out. Back then you didn't have the highway department to come and fix every road. Folks took care of stuff themselves. We had the road passable, but it still had some muddy spots and you know how that red Alabama mud can take a while to dry out. We had been working steady through the morning. At lunch, mama brought us some corn pone, cane syrup, beans and buttermilk.

We generally didn't eat that good when out working, so after lunch we were all full and feeling good about getting a hard job done. We lit into working on the fence and had finished the last strand in a couple of hours. Daddy always wanted a good strong fence and this one was. We made sure every post was stout and every strand of barbed wire was tight. Daddy was going to plant peanuts in that field this year. He had heard of folks down around Dothan making good money on peanuts. After harvest, they let hogs in the field to fatten up on peanuts missed in harvesting."

June Bug was getting a little impatient and more than a little confused. "Grandpa, what does growing peanuts and having a good fence have to do with me busting Randall in the mouth?"

"I am just getting to that, Son, hold on." He paused to recollect himself. "We had just finished and were putting our tools away when Obadiah Watson come riding up.

"The Watson's settled in this area early. They were some of the first white people in this part of Alabama. Most of the early Watson's were good people, but along the way they have become the no-count, white trash they are today. Most folks say it started with Obadiah. On this day, Obadiah was out riding with a couple of his no-count cousins. Most likely they were up to no good. But, I will say this for Obadiah: he had an eye for horseflesh. All his life he had a good saddle horse. This day he was on a beautiful white stallion. The other boys were riding on a couple of poor-looking, old, plow horses. Well, Obadiah comes up to the muddy spot in the road, stops his horse, looks down, and then yells at my daddy, 'Hey, old man Baker! Open up that fence. I need to get through!'

"My daddy didn't even look at him, but said loud enough to be heard, 'You can ride on, the road is passable.'

"Obadiah gets all uppity and says, 'You don't ride a fine horse like this through a mud hole like that!'

"Daddy looks at Obadiah and says, 'Then turn around and go back the way you came.'

"Obadiah was not used to not getting what he wanted, when he wanted it. He got real mad, real quick. He jumped off his horse, got a pair of wire pliers out of his saddlebag and stomped over to the fence like he owned the place. As he walks up he says, 'I told you to open up that fence.'

"Daddy walks over and meets Obadiah at the fence. Obadiah puts the pliers on the top strand and grips them to cut. Daddy puts his left hand on Obadiah's hand.

"With a real firm, quiet voice he looks Obadiah in the eye and says, 'You cut that wire and somebody is going to die.'

"That's when I slid my hand in my pocket where I kept my .32 revolver. Out of the corner of my eye, I could see that Leon had his hand in his pocket. I couldn't see Lynard, but I knew he would be doing the same. Obadiah was red-faced with anger. The two cousins were just sitting on their horses looking kinda' shocked. I could see that the closer one had a pistol in a holster on his right hip, but his right hand was holding the reins of his horse. The other cousin was sorta' behind Obadiah from where I stood, so I could not see how he was armed. He was closest to Leon. If that wire were cut, Leon would shoot him in a flash. If Obadiah cut that wire, I decided to shoot the man on horseback that was closest to me. Obadiah's right hand was held by daddy's left hand, which would slow him down if he reached for a gun. By the time he got it out, Lynard would have shot him once maybe twice, and who knew what daddy would do.

"There was a long silence and nobody moved or even breathed for all I could tell. Then Obadiah commenced cussing daddy. Called him everything and used words I had never heard before, but I assumed they was curse words. He pulled the pliers off the fence, got back on his horse and let fly more cussing. Leon was so mad about the way daddy was being cussed that he was twitching to shoot, but daddy just put his hand on Leon's shoulder and soothed him down a little.

"Daddy stood there watching while they rode off. Then daddy looked at us and said something I'll never forget and don't you forget it either. He said, 'A good man has always got to be a little tougher than a bad man.'"

June Bug looked at Grandpa Lymon, "You mean I got to be a little tougher than Randall?"

"That is right, Son, Randall is a bad boy and you will have to be a little tougher than he is."

To June Bug, it seemed impossible that his sweet and gentle old grandfather had ever held a pistol ready to shoot someone. And it seemed that standing up to Randall by himself was just as impossible. It would be a lot different than standing up to someone when you have them out numbered.

"If I punch Randall in the mouth, I will get in all kinds of trouble. I don't want to think of what mama and daddy will do to me, not to mention getting put out of school."

"That is true. You will get in some trouble, but my guess is it won't be much. And if you don't stand up to him you will live with trouble. Trouble don't go away on its own. You just pick what is right and take the trouble that comes with it."

June Bug's concentration wasn't that great the next morning in class. He had made up his mind that he would stand by Terrance and if that meant getting the fool beat out of him after he punched Randall in the mouth, then so be it. But his resolve still didn't keep him from thinking about it.

After lunch, he and Terrance got up from the lunch table and Terrance started toward the front hall, the long way to biology class. "No, Terrance, we going out the regular way," June Bug said.

"June Bug, maybe we ought to avoid Randall for a few days. Give it a little time."

"Terrance, we walkin' down the back hall today and any day we feel like it."

Terrance, reluctantly but faithfully, walked with June Bug. Sure enough, there was Randall Hardy standing in the way. He waited till Terrance got close and said, "I told you not to come this way. This is going to cost you, boy." He put a lot of emphasis on that last word.

"You touch him and I'll bust you in the mouth with all my might," June Bug said, trying to sound like his Great Granddad he never knew.

"Shut up, Bug, or I will crush you, too."

"You are not touching Terrance and that is all there is to it." For the first time, June Bug noticed that the hallway was a lot more crowded than usual.

From somewhere off to his left and a little behind Randall, Dwight Thomas piped up. This was before Dwight and June Bug stopped being friends. Dwight said loud enough for everyone to hear, "You punch him, June Bug, and I will cut him." Randall and Dwight Thomas had hated each other a long time and Randall had beaten Dwight up a few times. Nathaniel Jones stepped up and stood by Terrance. They were cousins and nobody doubted that Nathaniel wouldn't let Terrance get hurt.

Randall knew he was in trouble. Dwight was just crazy enough to cut someone and June Bug was not going to back down. Trying to find a way to get out with his dignity intact, Randall puts his index finger in the middle of June Bug's chest and said, "You all tough when you got friends around. Well, I'll come back with my friends."

A girl's voice spoke up, "Randall, you ain't got no friends. Nobody likes you, anyhow." That brought a roar of laughter and Randall stomped off in a rage just as Mr. York, the shop teacher, came around the corner telling folks to break it up and get to class.

"June Bug," Terrance asked, "did you plan all your back up or are you just a little crazy squaring off with somebody like Randall?"

June Bug looked at Terrance and with a sparkle in his eye said, "It is like this, Terrance. A good guy has got to be just a little tougher than a bad guy. Now, let's go to class."

CHAPTER 12

The Right Hand of Fellowship

G randpa Lymon had stopped being an elder at the Cambridge Church. He said he was too old to go visiting like an elder should. But he did stay involved with the church and helped out, as he was able. One year during fall revival, his diplomacy and gentle way helped bring a wayward sheep back to the fold.

The way it happened was this: Monday night after the first night of the revival folks were standing around talking and Pastor Mann said, "Tom Watson has not come to revival and, come to think of it, has been out of church for the last couple of weeks. I think we ought to go see if all is well." A number of folks commented that Tom hadn't been in touch with anybody for a while.

The guest evangelist, Roy Hay, who was a true man of God and who had a heart for lost sheep like few other preachers said, "Tell me where he lives and I will go visit him."

Grandpa Lymon who was standing there visiting with folks offered his two cents, "You not being known probably shouldn't go about looking for a Watson by yourself. It might cause trouble. I think it would be better if me and Pastor Mann were to go and we would be proud to take you along with us."

Grandpa Lymon had a special interest in Tom Watson. Most of the Watson's were no-count to some degree or another. A few of them made good, but by and large, they were a family of no-count, drinking, fighting, and cheating white trash. Tom or Thomas Stonewall (yes, his middle name was Stonewall-all the Watson's named their boys after Bible characters or Confederate generals) was as tough as any Watson comes. He was noted for being a fighter, a good hand with a gun, and the best hunter among any of the Watson's. But he was best known for his cussing.

It was said Tom didn't have to tan hides with salt he would just cuss them dry. It was claimed that Tom once cussed a sailor so bad the sailor was seen taking notes on how to cuss. These things weren't true, but Tom could cuss like no one else in all McComb County. He had, by and large, avoided the drinking vice, which may have been the only vice he didn't engage in. Unlike most Watson's, Tom was a hard worker, but he tended to be a bit of a loner. Tom's work ethic kept him from fitting in with his Watson kin. And being a Watson kept him from fitting in with anyone else. So, Tom mostly kept to his farm, which was productive and he kept the place clean unlike most Watson's. Besides farming, Tom worked as a pulpwooder, which suited his solitary disposition.

Tom traded at Grandpa Lymon's store and was the only Watson who had never asked for credit. Watson's were not known for being friendly and Tom was no different. Nevertheless, Tom and Grandpa Lymon had built up some respect for each other. Over time Tom and Grandpa began having conversations about life, family, right and wrong and ultimately faith. Year before last, Tom brought his family to Cambridge Church for Mother's Day and a few weeks later Tom became a Christian. Tom asked to be baptized in the river being that was how Jesus was baptized. Some folks were concerned that when Tom's sins were washed away it might kill every fish clean down to the Gulf.

The change in Tom's life was evident to everyone. He was a might more joyful and friendly. He would speak to people on the occasions he was in town. He and his family never missed church or Bible study. He was known to have taken up Bible reading and would even help folks out a might, which was unheard of for a Watson. But the biggest change was he stopped cussing. That was what folks noticed most.

Occasionally, ornery folks would try to get him to cuss. One day, Tom was in the gas station spending a little time socializing. When he came out to get in his truck he reached in the window to open the door 'cause the outside handle was busted. Well, a couple of the boys had put a mousetrap on the handle. When he reached in that trap snapped on his fingers. That scared Tom good-didn't hurt- just startled him. Ol' Tom got a look in his eyes and everybody just knew he was going to cuss a blue streak. But Tom held back and looked at the two boys off by themselves laughing and he simply said, "I'm going to pray for you boys." Yep, no doubt about it, Tom was a changed man.

That is why Tom's missing church for a couple of weeks made Pastor Mann a little concerned, but worse than that, Tom had promised to come to the revival meeting and his not showing up indicated that something was wrong. It was decided that Pastor Mann, Grandpa Lymon, and the Revival preacher would head out to Tom's place about noon the next day. Tom generally took lunch at home, so it was a good guess that he would be there.

The road out to Tom's place was little more than a wide, dirt path. The tree limbs reached over the road and were shaped as if a pulpwood truck was used to trim them. There was no driveway at Tom's place. There was a wide turn around with a truck loaded with pulpwood and a white, Ford Falcon, station wagon at the end of the road, and next to it a path up the hill and into the woods. Up that path a hundred yards or so was a little, three-room cabin. Brother Hay would later say, "If you have ever seen the TV show Beverly Hillbillies you have some idea of what the house looked like." He was, of course, referring to the house in Tennessee not Beverly Hills. Two lazy dogs were under the front porch. They barked a couple of times, but made no effort to get up. The three men of God mounted the four steps to the porch and Pastor Mann knocked.

Tom opened the door about four inches and in a voice as surly as any Watson ever used asked, "What you fellers wanting?"

Pastor Mann answered, "Brother Tom, we have come to see you."

"Well, you seen me now."

Grandpa Lymon spoke to Tom, "Can we come in and talk for a minute?"

For a moment it seemed that Tom would ask them to leave. He seemed to be vacillating between two choices. But he opened the door and stepped back to offer less than hospitable admittance. They stepped into the front room that had a small couch to one side, a dinner table to the other with a kitchen beyond that. It was clean, but simple and smelled of collard greens.

Once the door was closed, Pastor Mann asked, "May we sit down?"

Tom's jaw was set hard, no hint of humor, and his countenance was a cross between anger and impatience. "I reckon you can talk standing."

Grandpa Lymon spoke up next. He was on friendly enough terms to be very direct with Tom. "Tom, what is ailing you? Why are you acting so cross?"

That was all Tom needed. The pent-up emotion was set free. He withheld his cussing, but his voice was filled with hurt and disappointment. "You don't do what the Bible says you are supposed to do!"

Pastor Mann, who seemed to be as relaxed as one of those dogs under the front porch, asked, "Well, Tom, what does the Bible say we are supposed to do that we haven't been doing?"

"The Good Book says you are supposed to visit folks when they are in jail and when I was in jail not a soul from the church came to visit me."

At this point, Brother Hay was looking a bit out of sorts. He was from a large, big city church. His was a wealthy congregation that was only vaguely aware of the life of the rural poor. Beyond that he was accustomed to polite society and was not used to dealing with folks like the Watson's.

But Grandpa Lymon was nonplussed, "What happened, Tom. Why were you in jail?"

Tom hesitated a moment, the emotions welling up inside of him seemed to be fighting to come out, perhaps violently. "Well, it was that nephew of mine. Nadab is my second cousin and his boy, Hebron, has been riding his motorbike through my garden, been doing it since spring. Well, I told Nadab and Hebron both that I wanted him to stop. I did what the Good Book said about a gentle answer turning away wrath. But might as well been talking to a stump.

"Well, few weeks ago I go down into Dallas County to Orrville to get a part for my tractor. As I was getting out of my truck Hebron comes by on his motorbike. I think he followed me down to Orrville just to be a pestilence. Anyhow, he come riding up behind me and as he goes by slaps me on the back of my head and then takes off in a hurry. So, I reach in my truck, pull out my pistol and shoot him a might."

Brother Hay blurted out a question he never really meant to ask, "Did you kill him?"

Tom looked at Brother Hay with a somewhat bemused expression-like he might have been from another planet or maybe had an extra head. "No. Didn't aim to kill him. Just creased him a bit." Here he drew his finger across the left side of his waist. Tom was the kind of marksman that could put a bullet anywhere he wanted. He shot Hebron right where he aimed to shoot him. "Anyhow, the sheriff came down, took me off to jail and gave me an arrest paper."

"Well, Tom," Pastor Mann spoke slow and easy, "we had no idea you were in jail. This is the first I heard about it."

"Tom, I would have come down to see you if I had known and would be proud to do it." Grandpa Lymon added. "Why didn't you let us know? We want to know things like that."

Tom choked up a little and his voice broke as he spoke, "I was ashamed for what I had done. I was ashamed that I had brought embarrassment on the church after the church had been so good to me. I was afraid that the people of the church would think that I was just acting like a white-trash Watson. I was afraid Jesus might take back my baptism." Tears rolled from the corners of his eyes across a leathery, wrinkled face.

Grandpa Lymon placed his arm about Tom's shoulder, "Jesus ain't taking back your baptism, Tom. He ain't interested in finding a reason to throw you out. He wants to pull you in. You know that song we sing, *What a Friend We Have in Jesus*? Friends like Jesus don't give up on you and I won't either."

"Tom, you need your church family now. You don't need to worry about anybody saying anything. Everybody in that church has got some dirt all over them. Even Brother Lymon has got dirt on him," Pastor Mann said with a smile. "And, Tom, if anyone does say something to you or about you, I will deal with it personally."

"Tom," Brother Hay finally spoke again, "do you remember the story of Jesus washing the disciple's feet?" Tom acknowledged that he did. "Well, he washed their feet, but later he said they were clean. Why do you think he said that?"

"I don't know, Preacher. Never really thought about it."

"Well, it is 'cause even a clean man gets his feet dirty walking on a dirt road. Even a good man like brother Lymon here gets a little dirt and sin on him living in this old world. We all do. But Jesus keeps cleaning us up. There is nothing to be ashamed of, getting dirty, but it is a shame to stay that way."

Tom was real quiet. He was thinking hard about what they were saying. He seemed to come to some resolution. "That does make sense."

Sensing a mood change, Brother Hay asked, "Tom, if you don't mind my asking, how did you got out of jail?"

"Well, when I told the judge what happened and about Hebron riding through my garden, he said, 'Sounds like he needed shooting' and he let me go. I guess he knows Nadab and Hebron."

"Since you're out, you ought to come to revival meeting tonight. The church won't hold anything against you, Tom." Brother Hay said.

After a long pause Tom spoke up, "I reckon we'll come. You can expect us."

Good as his word, that night at revival Tom and his wife and kids were in their regular seats. They sang with the hymns and listened closely to the preaching. And when the sermon was over, Pastor Mann got up and invited those who were willing to come forward as they sang "Just as I am", Tom walked down the aisle. When the congregation sang the words, "I come" and the music stopped Tom spoke up.

"Some of you may have heard I broke the law and went to jail. It is true. I shot Hebron Watson."

At this point, someone in the church house said, "Amen."

"I am here to say I am sorry for what I did and any shame I brought on this church or you good people." Tom didn't hang his head in shame or look like a man that was trying to avoid something. He simply looked out on the audience, looking the congregation in the eye.

Brother Hay was still standing in the pulpit where he had preached. He spoke up, "No one in this congregation can throw a rock at this man. He did wrong, but he is sorry to God for it and that is a good start. We are going to sing a second verse and while we sing those of you who are willing I want to come up here and offer Tom the right hand of fellowship. Let's sing."

The words "Just as I am" were hardly sung, when the good folks of the Cambridge Church began to walk down to shake hands with Tom. Every man, woman and child shook hands with

Tom and more than a few gave him a hug. He was fully restored to good standing in the hearts of the people.

Tom later apologized to Hebron and Nadab, but that didn't go as well. He took Grandpa Lymon with him to give some moral support. After he said his piece, both Nadab and Hebron cussed Tom out, but Tom just stood there without saying a word. When they were done and before he walked away he said, "I'll be praying for y'all."

And just for the record, he never shot anyone again; whether they needed it or not.

CHAPTER 13

How June Bug Got the Nickname "Hootie"

Seemed like everybody knew Deroy Johnson Jr. as "June Bug". But for a very short time, he was also known as Hootie. His dad's name was Deroy, so that explains where Jr. came from. His momma was the one who started calling him June Bug. Maybe it was because he was born in June, or maybe it was because as a youngn' he was always buzzing around her like a June bug on a string. Some people said it was because he looked like a June Bug, but nobody ever said that more than once (at least not to his face). Why his mama called him June Bug was an unsolved mystery. But the how he got his nickname "Hootie" is no mystery at all.

During the summer between 10th and 11th grade, June Bug went through a stage of sinful rebellion. It was a very short-lived venture into folly for June Bug. He was raised in a fine Christian home and he knew how to act, but as is sometimes the case with teenagers, June Bug started acting up. It started with him running around with some no-count, white-trash people-some of the Watson cousins and their kin. First noticeable change started with him getting a real sassy mouth. June Bug was, on occasions, goofy, but this behavior was not childish folly. He was growing rebellious. But the real worry was he started doing some drinking, never fallen-down drunk, but drinking all the same. Besides it being illegal, it broke his mama's heart on account of her brother Sherman. On top of that, his drinking put him and his daddy in a bad way.

Grandpa Lymon was concerned, but he refused to be anxious about it. He told Deroy and Carolina, "That boy will come around. It may take him a while, but he will come around. 'Bring up a child in the way he should go, and when he is old he will not depart from it.'"

Not many folks knew what was going on, but those that did knew big trouble was coming unless the Lord moved in one of His mysterious ways. That is what his mama prayed for, and that is precisely what the Lord did.

It happened right after cotton harvest in the late summer. June Bug was out with some of his no-count, white-trashy friends on a Friday night. He was all proud 'cause he had taught his pet rat, named Gene Simons, a trick. June Bug's mama believes to this day that pet rat was part of the evil in June Bug's life, seeing as to how he started acting up about the time he got the varmint. Anyhow, June Bug had taught the rat to stand on his hind legs perched up on his shoulder. He would give it a peanut at the same time playing *Freebird* by Lynard Skynard on his 8-track player. After a while, every time the rat heard that song he would stand up. June Bug was out with his trashy friends playing *Freebird* and giving the rat peanuts when the boys started drinking.

Somewhere along the way somebody said, "We are not being very neighborly to Gene," speaking of Gene Simons the rat. "If he will stand up for a peanut, no telling what he would do for a beer."

One of the white-trash Watson's said, "I know I'll do more for beer than for peanuts."

Using a bottle cap as a makeshift cup they began giving the rat little drinks of beer. For his part, June Bug joined in. Before long Jung Bug and Gene both had a pretty strong buzz going. Gene was a loud drunk. Some drunks get affectionate, some get mean, and some get docile. Gene got noisy, hung on to June Bug's shirt and sang up a storm. At least he thought he was singing. To everyone else, it was just the annoying sound of a squeaking rat. Which explains why June Bug had to walk home that night. Nobody in his right mind is going to get in a car with a drunken rat.

The boys were way out at Bear Creek Woods and it was a good five miles back home by road, but not nearly so far as the crow flies. So, June Bug decided to cut across the corner of the woods and through the little black community known as Creekside and get himself home a lot faster that way.

June Bug was just out of the woods and getting close to Creekside, but he was also getting pretty miserable. First, he was tired of having a rat squeaking in his ear; that stunt is only funny so long. Not only that, his conscience was bothering him a good bit. He knew when he got home his mama would be worried, and then mad, and then she would start crying. His daddy would show disappointment in his eyes and would take him to the woodshed for a talk and corrective measures. On top of everything else, June Bug knew what he was doing was wrong. He knew Uncle Sherman Baker was a drunk and mama was afraid he would end up like her brother Sherman, living life either in jail or squatting in some old abandoned farm shack or something.

June Bug stopped for a moment. He could hear church music from somewhere in Creekside. He stood real still trying to hear the music over the sound of Gene. As he stood there in the first cool after a summer day, all his thoughts and feelings were spinning around in his heart just waiting for something to make sense of it all. He stood there very still and quiet trying to think about what he was going to say when he got home, why he was doing what he was doing and if maybe he needed to get a better class of friends. At this moment of contrition, the Lord moved in His mysterious way.

Gene Simons' singing had not gone unnoticed. A big, 'ole, horned owl decided he would take that rat for dinner. Between the last minute's reaction of Gene and June Bug stumbling over a root and when something brushed him, the owl managed to get one set of talons into Gene and the other tangled into June Bug's shirt and skin. At this moment, Gene wasn't the only one making noise. June Bug was convinced that the demon of strong drink was about to drag him off to eternal punishment. Now before you get all uppity, remember this boy's conscience is bothering him and is still a little addled from the drink. He has just walked out of the dark woods and it is full dark.

June Bug took off running and the first place he came to in Creekside was the All Saints Great Pisgah African Methodist Episcopal Church. Every church had revival after cotton harvest. It has been that way forever. Even back to slave days, after cotton harvest, the slaves would have a little break and they would have prayer meetings. That tradition was passed down from generation to generation and it was an especially festive time for a black church. At the moment, June Bug did not have any concern for racial profiling; he was just looking for a place with people, any people. He came charging toward the church with a screaming rat on his shoulder and an angry owl tangled in his shirt and convinced by this time, it is the devil himself who had him.

Worship in a black church can be noisy, but June Bug's presence took it to an all new level. He busted through the doors yelling and screaming. There remains some dispute what he was saying as he made his entrance. The bright florescence lights were not to the owl's liking, so he was more motivated than ever to let go of his supper. June Bug headed down the center aisle, got to the kneeing bench, made a hard-left turn and in this way began running a lap inside the church. It was as he completed the first lap almost exhausted, when the owl extricated itself from June Bug's shirt and, still holding Gene, launched itself toward an open window.

June Bug fell to the hardwood floor in front of the altar, panting, crying, and asking Jesus to forgive him. If there is a place in all the world to fall to the floor panting, crying, and asking Jesus to forgive, it is at the altar of the All Saints Great Pisgah AME Church. No sooner was that owl out of the window than the singing resumed and the attendants were there ministering to June Bug, fanning him with hand-held, funeral home fans, praying over him and putting a pillow under his head.

June Bug later recalled that he had a hard time remembering what happened, "It was all kind of jumbled up in my mind. I just remember a lot of friendly, dark faces looking at me. It did feel warm and safe. That is what I remember most-feeling warm and safe."

Later that night, out on the screened in fellowship hall, June Bug was talking to Pastor Horace Jones. "Pastor Jones, what am I going to say to mama and daddy?"

Brother Jones (that is what everybody called him) spoke in that deep, baritone voice that must have sounded like God's own voice. "Son, you tell 'em you sorry to them and to God. That's all you say. Then you live like you know you supposed to live. 'Even a child is known by his actions, by whether his conduct is pure and right.' If you live right, everything will be all right. And if you ever think about drinking again, you just remember that 'ole Hootie Owl and that will set you right."

That is how June Bug got the nickname Hootie. A nickname he wasn't real proud of, but one he answered to all the same.

CHAPTER 14

Who Needs a Key When You Can Use a Hammer?

H is name was Dwight Thomas, but for a while everyone called him CB. The letters CB were in no way associated with his name. That was the nickname that was applied to him because of the way he talked. When citizen band radios became the craze, CB jumped on that bandwagon early. His car may not have been worth $300, but if it was, two-thirds of the value was in the CB radio. As soon as he got one installed in the car, he started saving for a base station for his room. That way, he explained, he would not have to sit in the car at night to talk to people. To talk with CB in person was to enter a world of incoherent gibberish, unless you happened to spend a lot of time listening to truckers talk on their radios. CB's entire vocabulary slowly began to shift to a collection of slang and 10-code. The result was that a great many people could not understand him at all.

It got so bad that CB's dad was called to school regarding CB's language. It happened on Friday morning in homeroom. CB started in, "Breaker, Breaker, there, OL, this the Thunderbolt riding in the rocking chair. I need to change my 10-20 for a 10-100 come on back with a big 10-4, good buddy." Roughly translated that comes out as, "Excuse me, Teacher, (OL actually means old lady, but CB was improvising) I am Dwight Thomas. I am in my proper seat (rocking chair was actually a middle truck in a convoy of truck exceeding the speed limit), but I need to leave the room and go to the restroom. Please say, 'yes'." Good buddy was a reference to almost anyone. Once she had translated, Mrs. Cox sent CB to the bathroom and then to the office. CB's dad, who left work to deal with this little issue, was direct, forceful, and spoke a language CB would understand. He knew how to communicate with CB.

"Breaker, Beaker, this is Big Dad looking for that ankle biter, Thunderbolt. You got your ears on, good buddy? Good buddy, there is a bear trap set for you and smoky is just itching to be a paperhanger on you. So, you better watch your back door 'cause you don't want a gumball machine lightening you up. You copy that, Thunderbolt?" Mr. Thomas oversaw shipping at the gin mill, so he knew how to talk citizen's band.

Translation: "Are you paying attention, Dwight? The principal of this school has had enough and is ready to bring swift punishment. One more mess up and you are in serious trouble. Do you understand?"

Then in a dad voice that causes every kid to get really scared, Dwight's daddy said, "You talk any more nonsense and I will whip you with a briar." Now, I don't recall any one ever actually getting a whipping with a briar, but the thought of a briar rather than a hickory switch was enough to cause an immediate change of behaviors. "Are we clear about this, Son?" Dwight replied, "10-f.... I mean, yes, Sir." That ended CB's slang conversations at school, but his friends still had to suffer through his second language.

How he got his name has nothing to do with the story, but it will help to explain the communication the night of momentary stupidity on the point of two, 16-year-old boys. CB and June Bug had gone to a basketball game down in Monkey Town. (Montgomery) CB drove his pregnant, roller skate (a VW bug) and had deep and meaningful communication with truckers about the price of "go juice" (diesel fuel), the location of bear (law enforcement) taking pictures (using a radar gun) and the presence of a hungry heifer (an older lady looking for a man) at a local truck stop.

Honestly, June Bug found the slang tiring and found the best way to deal with it was to talk about a subject for which there was not a lot of citizen's band language available. He kept steering the conversations toward the game, or the Christmas party their parents were attending or some subject related to school. Even then, June Bug had to endure an occasional, "Put the Hammer Down" (push the accelerator to the floor) which had become an interjection of excitement for CB. June Bug's and CB's dads worked together at the gin mill and they were with their wives attending a Christmas dinner. That meant CB and June Bug could have a little freedom and they decided to spend it going to an away basketball game. The plan was simple, CB drove his parents over to the Johnson's, the two sets of parents would ride to the dinner together while the boys went to the game. The boys would get home before the parents and wait at the Johnson's house and then CB would ride home with his mom and dad. June Bug was thrilled because Martin Lee and Katie Debra were spending the night with Grandpa Lymon, so he didn't have to babysit them.

Well, CB and June Bug got home all right, but that was when the trouble started. June Bug left his house key in his room. (He would have forgotten his ears, but they were attached to his head.) June Bug checked all the windows and doors and everything was locked tight. Being a cold winter, the house was closed up tight. CB asked June Bug, "What we going to do now, good buddy?" June Bug could feel the rise of trucker talk in CB's voice.

June Bug was usually pretty good with coming up with an alternative plan if things went wrong. "I'll leave a note on the door and we will go down to Grandpa Lymon's. He ain't far and when our folks get here they can call and we'll come home."

CB said, "Naw, your grandpa don't have a TV. If we get to a TV quick, we can still see Daisy." He was, of course, referring to the character on the Dukes of Hazzard.

June Bug got the idea that CB had a plan already, but he didn't want to hear his suggestion. Instead, he suggested, "Well then, let's leave a note and go to your house. We can come back when our parents get in."

"Naw, that will take too long and I don't have much gas and what I do have has to last me till next Friday. June Bug, I have got an idea that will solve our problem." With that, CB went over to his car, lifted the hood, pulled out a hammer and came back to where June Bug was standing.

"What you going to do with that hammer?" June Bug asked.

"Only this," and then 'ol CB busted a windowpane beside the front door. "Now we can get in," he said triumphantly.

"You, bonehead, you broke the window!" June Bug screamed.

"Yea, but we are in. It is your fault. If you hadn't forgot your key, I wouldn't have had to bust this window."

"You didn't have to break that window! You wanted to. Oh, my daddy is going to kill me for this."

"Just tell him I did it," CB said as he reached in and unlocked the door.

"I will and then we are going to die together." June Bug practically spat.

"Your daddy won't hurt me." CB was supremely confident as he hit the palm of his hand with the hammer.

"Remember, bonehead, who is with my daddy tonight. In a few minutes, your dad will do the killing for my daddy."

The color drained from CB's face as he realized the scene that would greet his daddy. "We better clean this up pretty quick." CB felt that clean folly might reduce the length and severity of the beating.

June Bug had just taped a bit of cardboard over the empty pane when the parents arrived.

Deroy Sr. and Mr. Thomas were still a ways off when Deroy Sr. asked, "What happened?" Two teenage boys standing in a doorway with a hammer while the Dukes of Hazzard was on TV is a sure sign of trouble. Then both boys began to blurt out the story, each in a way that minimized their guilt. When it was over, it seemed that the two women folk were covering up laughter, but the dads were not amused.

"June Bug, you forgot your keys again? How about I put a logging chain around your waist and hook the keys to that? Boy, what do you think pockets are for?" exclaimed Deroy Sr. June Bug just kind of looked at the ground and said something about hiding one in a tree just in case.

Mr. Thomas was by far the more upset, "Let me get this right. You thought that busting a window was a better solution to being locked out than leaving a note and waiting for us at Grandpa Lymon's? Boy, what in the world......ah...ehh." Finally, his words trailed off to nothing and he turned to Mr. Johnson.

"Deroy, I am sorry about this. He will pay for it."

"Daddy, I ain't got no money."

"Yea, you do, boy. The money you are saving for that CB base station will be more than enough to buy a window. If need be, you will sell that CB out of your car. If that don't work, I will take it out of your hide. You apologize to Mr. Deroy and to June Bug."

"I'm sorry I broke out your window, Mr. Deroy. I realize it wasn't a smart thing to do. Sorry, I didn't listen to you and then got you in trouble, June Bug."

Before either of the Johnson men could say anything, Caroline said, "Let's go in for a piece of pie. With the boys locked out at least we know they didn't eat it all." As they walked in Carolina put one arm on each of the boys' shoulders and said, "Just learn a lesson from this boys, 'The way of a fool seems right to him, but a wise man listens to advice.'"

The window got repaired, June Bug and CB continued to be friends for a while longer and, best of all and to everyone's delight, within a year CB gave up trucker lingo. And, in the greatest of ironies, years later became an English teacher.

CHAPTER 15

Catfish Noodling Ain't a Sin, but It Is not Real Bright Either

There may be some folks who don't know what Catfish Noodling is. It is something of a sport and something of a game where by the fisherman catches catfish by hand. Techniques vary but the principle is the same. You get in a deep creek or river where you know there are catfish and you feel along the bank looking for an underwater cave or hole. Once you find a hole or a cave, you run your hand up in that hole feeling for a catfish. When you find that catfish, you tickle 'em under his mouth or chin. Usually, the fish will open his mouth up and when he does, you slip your hand inside and grab ahold of its lip and then pull the catfish out. The big advantage to this kind of fishing is it doesn't matter if the fish are biting or not, you are the one doing all the catching. But there are some disadvantages to noodling catfish.

Catfish noodling ain't a sin, but some folks look down on it as if it were. June Bug was never very big on noodling, not that he was scared, but it just seemed like the hard way to get a fish. He was of a mind that if you wanted to get fish, why not use a hook and line? If you need lots of fish quick there were other ways. You could always pour bleach in the water. That would send the fish to the top quick where you could dip net 'em out. Some folks used a hand-cranked generator to shock the fish and the old timers talked about blasting the water with dynamite. Light a stick of dynamite and chuck it in the water and after it exploded, fish would just float up. Dynamite was getting hard to come by so not many folks did that anymore, but rumor was 'ole man Brown did the same thing with black powder and a bit of hose pipe (sometimes called water hose). He would take a piece of hose pipe and pinch it double and tape it up real tight. From the other end he would fill the pipe with powder, then pinch off the other end and tape it down. Finally, he would poke a hole in the hose and stick in some fuse. It was pretty much as good as dynamite. Mr. Brown was known to drink a little and when he drowned in the river it was assumed he blew himself out of the boat and wasn't sober enough to get back in.

Along the creeks and waterways feeding into the Alabama River, there were more than a few good catfish. June Bug had a friend, Harold, who loved to go noodling. He was convinced that he was the best noodler who ever lived and that one day noodling would make him rich and famous. However, he was kind of vague on how he thought noodling would make him rich and famous. Harold was so in love with noodling that he assigned himself a nickname. The problem with self-assigned nicknames is that they almost never stick. But Harold was determined and so, for a long time, he told people that he should be called "Catfish Hunter". Most folks thought it had something to do with the baseball player from North Carolina; others thought he was just a little crazy. His friends just called him Harold.

Harold came by June Bug's house one summer day and asked June Bug to go noodling. It was hot that day and June Bug was done with his chores and not having much else to do he went along. He kinda wanted to make sure Harold didn't get himself hurt or killed with some of his fool antics. On this particular day, Harold was more stirred up than usual. He claimed he had seen a catfish that was at least four feet long. Harold was known to get a bit carried away from time to time. Said he saw it just downstream from the milldam. He was planning on checking the banks of the creek down there till he found where that big 'ole boy was holed up. The creek was fast, but there were a few eddies where water circled and ran upstream for a few feet. It made the kind of place where Harold was convinced there would be holes in the underwater bank; deep enough for big fish, but not so deep that you would be in over your head. By the time they got to the creek Harold had worked himself into a tizzy about that fish.

June Bug said to Harold, "You better rein in your excitement, Harold. You may be getting into a peck of trouble."

"You might as well beat the rush and call me 'Catfish Hunter', 'cause that is what everyone is gonna call me after I get my picture holding this fish on the front page of the paper."

"I'll call you stupid if you get hurt down there in that creek. That creek bed ain't sand and clay; it's rocky there and you could slip and bust your head open. You don't know for sure how deep them eddy pools are and you could get caught in the current and be halfway to the Cahaba River before you know it."

"If you're scared, you can set up on the bank under a shade tree and look for rabbits."

To say someone was "looking for rabbits" was to say they were scared, even of rabbits. It was a pretty weak insult, but all the same June Bug was about to tell Harold he could hunt catfish on his own. Harold made an appeasing gesture and said, "I know things can go wrong. So, that is why I want you here. I got a rope in the bed of the truck you can carry. If I get in trouble, you toss it to me and pull me out."

They pulled up to the creek in a cloud of fine dust you can only experience on a hot, summer day. They made their way down to the creek and realized it was running faster than Harold recalled.

"Harold, this ain't smart." June Bug said.

But Harold, by this time, had done too much bragging to back out. He had to at least try. He worked his way down to an eddy where a big, old tree had fallen. The roots were pulled up and Harold figured the water would have washed out holes up in the bank and it would be a good place to start. Harold started poking around, not finding anything worth talking about. June Bug sat up on the bank holding the rope watching Harold splashing around and thinking Harold may be the dumbest friend anyone ever had.

Harold went down below the tree trunk and found what he called, "A cave with a mouth as big as my sister's" (Emma-Jean did have a big mouth). Harold was bent way over, about neck-deep with his hand up in that cave mouth, when he learned one of the great lessons of noodling. That lesson being: Catfish ain't the only critters that like underwater caves. That dawning moment of realization was accompanied by a sound that you would not expect to come from a 16-year-old boy. It was a sound somewhere between a squeal and a scream, maybe a closer resemblance to a grunt.

In a cave, you might find water snakes, including cottonmouths, crawdaddy's, and turtles and if the cave has an air pocket, beavers. No one ever knew for sure what Harold caught up in that cave; or rather, what caught Harold. Whatever it was, all of a sudden Harold found that he did not want to be a world-famous noodler anymore. At that moment, all he wanted was his hand back with all its parts still attached. Problem was, whatever had a hold of Harold felt safest by biting down and not letting loose. Harold commenced to pulling on his hand, but whatever had him bit down harder when he pulled. That thing was also braced against coming out.

He began yelling more understandably, "Help me, June Bug! Something's got me! Help me! Help me! It's goin' to eat me!!"

Not really sure what to do, June Bug tossed him the rope. But the last thing Harold wanted to do was to pull harder, so the rope just lay there in the water.

"Get down here and help!"

So, June Bug came tearing down the bank and got to the edge of the water, "What you want me to do?"

"Get down here and reach in there and grab that thing so it will let me go."

June Bug's mama would often say, "I didn't raise no fool," generally as a way of fussing at June Bug for doing something stupid. June Bug figured this would be a good time to prove his mama was right.

Under the best of circumstances, June Bug was not about to stick his hand up in a hole in a creek bank. He especially wasn't going to do it if he knows something biting is in there.

"Why don't you stick your other hand in there?"

"Come on, June Bug, help me." By now Harold was sounding pretty pitiful with his pleading.

June Bug had several different ideas rolling around in his head. He could just grab Harold and jerk him. He could go get some help. For the briefest of moments he thought about reaching in the hole and what he would do after that he had no clue. But after thinking for a second, each idea was discarded. Finally, with Harold's caterwauling getting worse, June Bug cut off a sapling stick and whittled a point on one end. All the while, Harold was getting more panicky by the minute. With the stick in hand, June Bug got down into the creek beside Harold and eased that stick up along Harold's arm till it was past his wrist. Then June Bug gave a hard poke. Whatever that thing was, it let go and Harold jumped back with his hand free. His hand was bit something awful, oozing blood from between the thumb and first finger. The wound looked worse than it really was, but at least all the parts were there.

June Bug helped Harold up to the truck and then got in to drive him home. On the way he asked, "What is your mama going to say?"

Harold replied, "I'm just going to clean and dress it without Mama knowing. If she asks what happened, I'll tell her I got hurt playing ball or something. She won't say anything. I get hurt a lot."

"I'll tell you what my mama would say, 'I didn't raise no fool.' Then she would quote that Bible verse she always quotes when I do something stupid: 'The prudent person sees trouble ahead and hides, but the naïve continue on and suffer the consequences.' You don't tell your mama and that hand will get infected and you will end up in big trouble. You tell your mama, 'Mr. Turtle Hunter', or I will."

Turtle Hunter (that's what June Bug called him from then on to get him riled) did tell his mama and she busted him on the side of the head then took him to see old Dr. King. Dr. King said he didn't need any stitches, but gave him a shot for tetanus. When Dr. King asked Harold what happened and Harold told him, the Doc started laughing and the more he thought about it the harder he laughed. He laughed till he was all red in the face and gasping for breath.

I wish I could say that was the last time Harold 'Turtle Hunter' Pratt did anything stupid, but it wasn't. However, he did from that day begin to think things through a little bit more and it was noticeable. Grandpa Lymon even commented, "That boy doth walk circumspectly when he has a mind to. And if Harold Pratt can do it, anyone can."

CHAPTER 16

How June Bug Married the Prettiest Girl in the County

B eth Ann was the prettiest girl at Robert Frost High School. She was the prettiest girl in all of McComb County. She would have been the prettiest girl in town if she had lived in Birmingham, Atlanta, or New York for that matter, but she didn't live there. Folks said she was just like her mama, but that may have been because nobody knew her daddy well. Her mama grew up just across the county line, but had lots of family in McComb so it was like she grew up there. After high school, she went to Ole Miss to study literature; she had aspirations of becoming an author. While there she met and married a young man in the ROTC. For their first anniversary, Mary Beth and William had a little girl. Then two years later, William Jr. came along. But as happened too often during the '60's, William was sent to Vietnam and he never came home.

As a widow with two little children, Mary Beth decided to move back home to be near her family and to raise Beth Ann along with her little brother, William Jr. Mary Beth never remarried-it was not that she was opposed to the idea-it was just that she was very scrupulous about what she expected. She said she "...would talk to men who were a quarter of the man her late husband was, be friends with any who were half the man he was, and marry any who came up to three quarters." She was polite to everybody and had more than a few suitors that wanted to keep company with her. But she could only name two or three men she actually considered friends and they were all married. She emphatically never dated anyone.

She wasn't opposed to Beth Ann dating; she was opposed to her dating no-count trash. She was a tender, attentive, and loving mom, but stern and hard as a hickory nut. Every boy in the county was afraid to try to date Beth Ann because of Miss Mary Beth. Rumor among the boys was that she was so mean her late husband volunteered to go to Nam just to get away from her. There were stories a lot worse than that, but there wasn't a bit of truth to any of them. Miss Mary Beth felt that she had to be imposing and severe like Beth Ann's daddy would have been. For her part, she was content to let the boys believe all the terrifying stories were true; it kept the no-count boys away from her daughter.

When Beth Ann complained about not having a boyfriend, her mama would tell her, "If you marry for fun, you will be bored. If you marry for money, you will end up a poor, old soul. If you marry for fame, you will end up ashamed. If you marry for pleasure, you will end up in pain. If you marry for power, you will end up fighting for control. But, if you marry 'cause God put a righteous man in your life, well, it is just beyond words."

Now, what has this got to do with June Bug? Well, June Bug's mama and Mary Beth were best friends having grown up together. When Mary Beth moved back to town, it was June Bug's mama that helped her the most. Mary Beth never grieved publicly, but in private it was Caroline who stood by her and even carried her. Over the years they taught Sunday School together, were in the church's ladies service circle together and whenever something needed doing at Mary Beth's house, June Bug's mama sent June Bug and his daddy to take care of it. June Bug cut the grass till William Jr. was big enough to do it himself. When June Bug suggested that, "Maybe I ought to get paid for cutting the grass," his mama's response was to say, "Maybe I ought to slap you nahkid (naked in case you didn't know), hide your clothes and send you off to school."

As Beth Ann grew up, there was one on-going battle that existed between her and her mama: the battle of wearing makeup. This battle began in about 7th grade and was fought off and on for the next several years. Mary Beth never had a lick of trouble from her daughter over anything excepting for wearing makeup. Mary Beth would not tolerate any sass or back talk, but they still had their moments of familial conflict. They finally reached a compromise that left both sides unhappy. Beth Ann could start wearing makeup beginning in the 11th grade, if she would stop pestering her mama.

Although Mary Beth and Caroline were best friends, Caroline thought this makeup ban was a bit much. Caroline had brokered this peace treaty. And when Beth Ann left the room with her unhappy victory, Caroline said, "Mary Beth, it seems to me that you are making a bigger deal out of makeup than it needs to be. A little paint never hurt an old barn." This was one of Grandpa Lymon's favorite sayings. Caroline was inserting it hoping a little humor would ease the tensions.

Mary Beth chuckled a little, "Are you saying my daughter is an old barn?" the lilt of her voice communicated that she was not angry. But there was no softening of her position. "Caroline, if my William were here to be Beth Ann's protector, to scare the living daylights out of any boy who came to call, who would know how a boy thinks, and protect my Beth Ann, I might be a little more willing to compromise. But it is just me. I am alone. I want to send a message to every boy she meets."

"You are not alone, Mary Beth. But what message do you think you're sending to Beth Ann?" That is all Caroline said. She, unlike a lot of folks, knew when to stop talking.

June Bug grew up with Beth Ann like she was a sister. They were really close and June Bug always took up for her. She was the only reason June Bug ever got in big trouble at school. Jimmy Parker had said some things about Miss Mary Beth that upset Beth Ann a whole heap. Beth Ann wouldn't say what it was, so June Bug went to Jimmy and told him to apologize. Jimmy said he wouldn't apologize 'cause everybody knew "it" was true. June Bug said he did not know what Jimmy was talking about. Jimmy told June Bug what "it" was. "It" had to do with the relationship between Deroy Senior and Miss Mary Beth. June Bug beat Jimmy so bad his mama would have had a hard time recognizing him. It would have been worse if the P.E. teacher hadn't been there. June Bug got sent home for a day. Jimmy was told to watch his mouth because the P.E. teacher might not be there next time. Funny thing was that when June Bug got in trouble at school he would get a whipping at home- except this time. All his daddy did was to tell him, "It is a wrongful thing to beat a man over what he says." June Bug had always been good to Beth Ann and they were always close. But mind you, June Bug had never even thought about asking to date her. Mary Beth's intimidation tactics worked on June Bug too; seeing as how he, like everybody else, would have to ask her mama for permission to even ask Beth Ann to go out.

Anyhow, June Bug was Beth Ann's best friend on earth. So, that is why it was not surprising that on the first day of Beth Ann's junior year, she would ask June Bug what he thought of her makeup. Having never had any makeup on in her life and her mama gone to work before Beth Ann put her makeup on, Beth Ann over did it a pinch. She was wearing more makeup than any four other girls put together. So, in she comes to the schoolhouse wearing a pretty new school dress, looking very grown up and her face covered with makeup. Some of the kids were talking and saying things that were not that nice. Some boys liked it for all the wrong reasons, some girls said unkind things and Beth Ann was feeling a little upset and unsure of herself. She came up to June Bug and said kind of serious and kind of pert, "June Bug, what do you think of my makeup?"

June Bug looked at her and he said, "You look like something from a science fiction movie and I ain't talking about the earthlings." Then June Bug looked right at her to see if she was going get mad or listen to him. She looked at him without moving a muscle or saying a word, so he figured it was okay to go on. "Beth Ann, you are the prettiest girl that ever lived and you don't need to be putting on." ("Putting on" is a complete statement and refers to a person attempting to have a pretense.) There's nothing wrong with makeup. You just don't need it." Then with a smile, he added, "But a little paint never hurt an old barn."

In the context of makeup, when a woman hears, "A little paint never hurt an old barn" there are typically two reactions. Some women get mighty upset and act like a setting hen being bothered, others laugh at themselves and some smile about it. Beth Ann was of the latter variety. Beth Ann said, "Do you mean that?"

"Course, I mean it. Paint never did hurt a barn." Then June Bug got really tense and without knowing what he was saying, his voice wavered a little and he went on, "Could I take you to a movie Friday night?"

Beth Ann smiled a smile that would shame an angel it was so bright. "You have to ask mama and if she says okay, I would love to go."

That night after supper, June Bug asked his daddy for the keys to the truck and explained why. Family rule was you didn't go out after supper on a school night, but Deroy made an exception. June Bug went over to Beth Ann's house and there was Miss Mary Beth sitting on the porch. June Bug always thought she was pretty, but at that moment more like a spider waiting on something. He came up and did what he is there to do. He asked permission to date Beth Ann.

"Miss Mary Beth, I would like to go with...I mean take Beth Ann to the movies this Friday, on a date with you, and um, with your permission, I mean." For a moment, June Bug had the overwhelming desire to throw up.

Miss Mary Beth sat there cool as a cucumber, not a flinch, not a stir. June Bug was beginning to think that he might ought to leave, not just the yard, but maybe the state of Alabama. Her eyes were looking like cold, hard, blue steel. "Deroy, Jr.," she never called him June Bug, "I always thought you were a good boy. I like you and your family. Beth Ann told me what you said this morning."

'Bout now June Bug was thinking he need not have come over at all, but he stood there brave as he could, which ain't saying much. Miss Mary Beth continued, "The Good Book says, 'An honest answer is like a kiss on the lips'. You were truthful to my Beth Ann. So, you can go out with her. But mind you, have her home on time and treat her right or one: I will tell your mama and two: whatever is left I'll..." and here she paused, maybe it was because she knew there wouldn't be anything left or maybe she was thinking of something really bad to do to June Bug or maybe she was pausing for effect, " ... I'll do to what is left of you all them stories you heard about what I did to my late husband. You understand me, Deroy, Jr.?"

"Yes, 'um."

"Come over for supper and then you all can go to the movie."

That is how it all began. June Bug never dated or even wanted to date anyone else. Most high school romances are nothing much but a bunch of empty talk and raging hormones, but Beth Ann and June Bug were different. It was like they never stopped being best friends. A few years later, June Bug stood in the same spot in front of the porch and asked to marry Beth Ann; still the prettiest girl in the county. June Bug's folks couldn't have been happier. June Bug felt like his mama and daddy liked Beth Ann more than him. He got that feeling from the little hints they would drop.

Like the time his daddy told him, "She is way better than you deserve, boy!" then his mama chimed in, "By a long shot."

June Bug always treated Beth Ann like a lady and a queen. Even in his worst moods he was kind and good to her. Like the time she backed his truck into a tree and put a big dent in the tailgate. He stood there a long time looking at it. Beth Ann was afraid he was going to be terribly mad, but instead his only comment was, "It looks like it's smiling." On occasions like this, Miss Mary Beth would speak up for June Bug and tell Beth Ann, "I do believe God put a righteous man in your life."

CHAPTER 17

"I Don't Think You Know What That Means"

Sally Wade was one of the sweetest, most innocent, and on at least one occasion, the funniest girl in all of Robert Frost High School. Sally's family was a fine, upstanding family that had been settled in the county right after The War. Her daddy, John Wade, ran the family farm, which was a very big farm. He was also a well-known leader in the community. He was on the deacon board of First Baptist, was a past president of the Peanut Growers Co-Op, active member of the Cattlemen's association, and a strong, financial supporter of the Fellowship of Christian Athletes and Fellowship of Christian Students. Her mama was equally upstanding and respected, as a member of the Daughters of the American Revolution and Daughters of the Confederacy. The only person near the standing of Grandpa Lymon for upstanding character in all McComb County, who wasn't a preacher, would have to be Mr. John Wade.

To give you an idea of how seriously John Wade took his convictions, he bought a TV with a remote, when they were considerably expensive, just so he could turn the TV off if a beer commercial came on. If a beer commercial came on TV, he would just turn it off and count to about a minute would go back and turn on the TV. Watching football games on Sunday afternoon was a lot easier when he didn't have to get up and turn the TV off by hand for every commercial break. Agree or disagree with him, everyone was confident of John's moral stature. It was his well-known character that made what Sally said so funny.

Sally was the same age as June Bug and was in his American History class in the 11th grade, which allowed June Bug to be an eye witness to the funniest thing ever said in a history class. Now to understand American History from the perspective of an Alabama classroom, you have to have a sense of proportions. Important things took up lots of time in class, while unimportant were just barely mentioned. So, it was not uncommon for a history teacher to spend a week on the discovery and exploration of the Americas and maybe up to two weeks on the events leading up the American Revolution and the Revolution itself. There would be a couple of days to cover westward expansion and the Trans-Continental Railroad, cowboys and the gold rush; three days for the First World War, a week for the Second World War, and one week for the years after World War 2. That is a total of 7 weeks. The balance of the year was spent on the War of Northern Aggression and the horrific aftermath. While that might not be an exact count of how much time was spent on the War, there was no doubt about it, that conflict was a major point of discussion in American history class. A radical Southern attitude about the war was expressed by CB. When he was in 11th grade, he decided that for an American history class project he would burn Abraham Lincoln in effigy. When asked, "Why?" he said, "Because the real Lincoln is dead and I can't burn him." His project proposal was rejected. While he may not speak for everyone, CB sort of sums up the passion southern folks have about The War.

During the study of the Civil War era, considerable time was spent talking about the institution of antebellum slavery. Every aspect of slavery was discussed in great detail, along with the implications for the post-war South, the Union, and contemporary

America. During one of the lessons about antebellum slavery, the history teacher Mrs. Lawrence talked about one of the more horrific tragedies of slavery. In deference to Sally's sheltered upbringing, Mrs. Lawrence was attempting to be especially tactful.

"There were some occasions, especially on some of the larger plantations, where certain female slaves were kept as concubines for the master. Now, does everyone know what that means?"

Sally spoke up as perky as you can please, "Yea, my daddy always keeps a couple of 'em, says he would like to have more, but they are really expensive."

A hush fell over the classroom, the stunned silence and the awkward stares must have tipped Sally off that something was wrong. She added apologetically, "He uses them to harvest the peanuts. Don't need them for anything else." To their credit, Sally's classmates did a good job restraining themselves. There was much stifled laughter and a lot of snickering. Sally looked around in confusion and inquired, "What?"

Mrs. Lawrence regained order with a word, but there was clearly a guffaw under her breath and she could hardly wait to repeat this story in the teacher's lounge. "Sally, I think you mean, 'combine.' That is not the same as a concubine." And with that, Mrs. Lawrence moved on to the next subject-the implication of the cotton gin and the role it played in increased slave population. Just before class ended Mrs. Lawrence asked Sally to step into the hall for a moment. When Sally came back in she was the color of a pickled beet. No one ever said anything to Sally about that, but everyone in that class had something to tell at the dinner table that night.

As it happened, Grandpa Lymon was over to June Bug's house for supper that night. He got a kick out of the story and then he recited the Bible verse, "A man hath joy by the answer of his mouth: and a word spoken in due season, how good is it!"

"What do you mean, Grandpa?" June Bug asked.

"The way little Sally spoke up means that girl never had a thought about the possibility of that wickedness. She could not imagine the kind of sinful things that folks used to do to each other. It is a funny thing the way it happened and all, but out of that girl's mouth comes the evidence that she is truly an innocent young lady. Would that more people were like that." Then Grandpa Lymon got kind of quiet.

Couple of weeks later, John Wade came in to Grandpa Lymon's store to pick something up and he came up to Grandpa and said, "Got time for a funny story, Lymon? Seems my little girl is a little confused about the difference between a combine and a concubine. It seems...."

CHAPTER 18

Why They Will Never Retire June Bug's Number ... at Least Not for Football

Robert Frost High School was never known to be a powerhouse in football. In fact, they only made the playoffs once every 5 to 10 years. Mostly, it was because the coaches were really teachers and not really football coaches. The coaches had played football in high school and a couple in college, but they were not focused on football the way a coach has to be in order to produce a consistently winning team. They loved the boys and were really busy having fun with their sport. They were not the high-pressure sorts of coaches you sometimes see. Being a small community and rural school, they were much better at FFA and hunting than sports. But they played every year anyway. Not a lot of Robert Frost "Poets" went on to play college ball. Nathaniel was the only prospect for college ball when June Bug played. June Bug and Nathaniel were captains their senior year-Nathaniel for offense and June Bug on defense.

June Bug had a great senior year. He played linebacker on defense and deep cover on special teams. He led the team in tackles, had two interceptions, a fumble recovery and three sacks. He was also the cheerleader for offense when he was not on the field. In a season with twice as many losses as wins it was easy to lose heart and hope. But June Bug kept it together. During games and at practices June Bug would say, "If you have lost hope, it's okay. I got enough hope for all of us." June Bug became a leader of men that year.

It had been a good season as far as Robert Frost High went. They entered the last game with three wins and six losses. That was more wins than the preceding three years combined. All three wins were in district play, meaning, if they won the last game they would go to the state playoffs.

This final game was a classic with both teams giving great effort, but showing why they only had six wins combined between the two of them. The game started badly for the Poets. They started the game by fumbling the first snap. Green County recovered the ball on the Poets' 18-yard line. June Bug led the defense on to the field telling 'em, "It don't matter; we can hold these boys." It was a valiant effort, but Green County scored anyway. By half time, the Poets were looking pretty beat down. They were down 13-0 (Green County had missed an extra point kick). But June Bug never stopped encouraging and cheering his teammates.

The second half opened with Green County scoring on their first possession. June Bug believed in his team even when down by 19 points. On the extra point attempt the snap went over the holder's head. When one of his teammates said, "I've given up hope," June Bug answered, "Well, I got enough hope for the both of us." June Bug refused to become dispirited. He would grab Nathaniel and tell him "Keep hitting the hole! Sooner or later it will open up." And it did twice, sure enough. Nathaniel scored on two, long runs of 45 and 32 yards.

Green County, having played a near perfect game in the first half, made up for it in the second half and began to show why they had lost six games in the season. They fumbled the ball, missed tackles and made silly mistakes,. Not that Robert Frost was playing mistake-free football but, in the second half, the mistakes just worked better for Robert Frost. It seemed that whoever made the last mistake would lose and, as you might guess, it was going to June Bug who made that mistake.

June Bug's toughest challenge of the season came at the end of the last game of the year. Not on the field, but after the game. Frost had fought its way to a 20–19 lead over Green County with less than a minute left in the game. Green County had the ball at midfield after a short Frost punt. On the first play of the drive, Green County connected on a deep pass and the wide receiver was pushed out of bounds at the 10-yard line. Facing a 1st and 10, a draw play up the middle advanced the ball six yards.

It was second and goal with the ball at the 4-yard line when June Bug called the defense to huddle, "We are going to do this as a team, win or lose. We are going to count on and trust each other. Stick to your assignments, trust your teammates and everything will turn out right."

The second down play was a pass that was knocked down at the line. Green County went with a no huddle trying to catch the Poets sleeping. They ran an option-pitch off the left side. June Bug was responsible for the quarterback on an option-pitch play. The quarterback waited too late to pitch the ball to the halfback and June Bug whooped him and the pitch went behind the running back. Four or five players were trying to get the ball and in the scramble, Green County recovered the fumble on the 22-yard line.

Facing a 4th and goal on the 22-yard line with five seconds left, Green County called a time-out to discuss their options. When they returned to the field they set up for a long field goal. The problem was they had the worst place kicker in the region, maybe the state. The reason they had 19 points was because they had already failed on two extra-point attempts that night, but only one of them was the kicker's fault. Coach Nobel called a time-out to ice the kicker and pulled over the defense. "Watch out for the fake. Don't worry about blocking the kick. Let the kicker do whatever he can. But don't let anyone get behind you or outside of you."

Neither Coach Nobel, June Bug, nor anyone else on the defense figured there was any way in the world they would actually attempt the long field goal. The boys from Green County were sure they were beaten; you could tell it by the way they came out on the field. Green County's coach had considered the game a lost cause as he called for a field goal attempt, but he acted all positive.

The snap was right, the spot was right on and the kick was awful. It pretty much went straight up and about 15 yards past the line of scrimmage. June Bug caught that ball like he was playing catch with his friends and began dancing and celebrating and running around. He ran up to Harold Pratt, spiked the ball and jumped in the air so Harold could catch him. The problem was the ball was still in play. When June Bug threw it down, it was nothing more than an intentional fumble. One of the boys from Green County picked it up, ran into the end zone, scored a touchdown and won the game. June Bug had made the last mistake of the game and cost his team a chance to play for a state title.

The Poets' were heartbroken; fans, students, parents, cheerleader, players everyone, but no one more so than June Bug. But a funny thing happened. June Bug expected to catch a lot of grief from the team, parents and coaches, but it didn't happen. The locker room was quieter than a funeral parlor on Halloween night until Nathaniel stood up. "June Bug that may be the worst football play I have ever seen, but at least it was made by one of best men I know. Anytime this season when I wanted to quit, you kept me going."

Harold spoke next, "June Bug, you picked me up a bunch of times, so I ain't going to let you get down on yourself."

Then one by one his teammates told June Bug how he had helped them during the season or at school or just around the county. June Bug couldn't say anything. He just sat there with a towel over his head and most of his face and cried real quiet-like. Coach Nobel stepped up and said, "Alright, boys, get cleaned up, but nobody leave. We walk out together tonight. We walk out as a team."

When everybody was about ready, June Bug was sitting off by the coach's office just waiting and trying to figure out how he could hide in the crowd as they left. Coach Nobel walked up to him and said, "June Bug, not a one of these boys will ever make a living playing football, especially you," with that he smiled his mischievous grin. "But, because of the leader you have become, all them boys," and he gestured to the locker room, "will know a little more about how to live. They respected you even when you failed because of the character you showed all year long. It is true what the Book says, 'Though God scoffs at scoffers, he gives grace to the humble. The wise will inherit honor, but he holds fools up for ridicule'. No one will say nothing to you; your teammates will see to that."

They never did retire June Bug's number, but they did talk about establishing the "June Bug Grand Spike Award" to be given to the most beloved player who really screws up. But nothing ever came of those plans. Green County went on to the playoffs and the next week lost 62–0 to the eventual state champ. Nathaniel got a scholarship to play ball at a little college where he went to study for ministry like his uncle Horace Jones. It took a while, but eventually June Bug got to where he could joke about that play. He began telling people, "You remember that last game where, on the last play, we called a trick play and everybody except me forgot what they were supposed to do?"

CHAPTER 19

Why CB and June Bug Stopped Being Friends

In much of the rural South there are two great holidays: the beginning of football season and the opening day of deer season. Deer hunting was a very big deal in McComb County, Alabama. Understandably, because deer hunting is a lot of fun, it can provide first-rate meat for the table, and to a bean farmer, a deer is a pest like a 150-pound rat. June Bug started hunting with his daddy before he could shoot. He shot his first buck by the time he was ten years old and hunted every chance he got. June Bug loved the fall of the year, but felt like the Lord should have made the hours of twilight longer 'cause that the best time for hunting.

There are two ways that folks in McComb County hunted: still-hunting and running dogs. When you still-hunt, you scout the area and look for places with deer signs. These places are where they rub their antlers on a small cedar tree or paw up the ground or something that indicated deer traveled there frequently. Near such a place, you put up a stand and wait for a deer to come by. When alone, June Bug would go sit in a tree stand a few dozen yards from a creek where the deer came and went from a thicket and would quietly wait for the deer to come by. Few things are more relaxing than watching the woods from a tree stand.

But June Bug also liked to run dogs. When running dogs, you had someone in a tree stand near a game trail where you expected deer to pass. Someone else would set dogs loose way up the holler or creek or into a thicket. The theory was the dogs would chase the deer down the game trail and past the hunter in the stand. The deer would pay so much attention to the dogs that they would come up on a hunter unaware of his presence.

There was a third way people hunted which, strictly speaking, was not legal. It is called deer shining. When you went deer shining you drove out to a field at night and used a spotlight to look across the field for deer feeding. When a deer looked at the light, it would freeze for a few seconds and then you could shoot it. Game wardens had a dim view of this activity and if they caught you, they would take and keep your gun, your truck, and would even arrest you. For this, and other reasons, June Bug never went shining.

One late fall on a Saturday, June Bug had a bad day of hunting. In the morning he was in the stand before daylight and he saw a beautiful buck. It was coming down a game trail and it carried a big rack. It had its head up high as he was moving. Rut was starting and the buck must have been scenting a doe. He was coming straight at June Bug. But all of the sudden he turned off the trail. He must have caught June Bug's scent 'cause it moved away before June Bug could ever get a shot. He caught a glimpse of it a couple of times, but never long enough to be able to draw a bead. Other than that, it was a completely quiet morning.

About 11:00, June Bug was getting hungry, so he got down out of his stand and went to the house. His daddy had to work that morning, so he didn't get to go hunting. When June Bug told him about the big buck he saw his daddy suggested, "We ought to try running the dogs after lunch. That deer will be bedded down and we might just stir it up and get a shot at it."

They had three hunting dogs. June Bug's dog was a two-year-old named Butch, which was short for Butcher. June Bug had a flair for the dramatic. While Butch was a good dog, he was a spoiled pet and he wasn't nearly fierce enough to be named Butcher. Their other two dogs were Midnight, a black lab that was crossed with a coonhound and Fluffy, a dog whose mama was a stray that Grandpa Lymon had taken in and her daddy was a stranger in the night. June Bug's mama named the dog Fluffy when it was pup. If she named it now, she might have named it Baldy. Deroy Sr. took the dogs in his truck and told June Bug he would give him plenty of time to settle in before letting them go up where the bean field met the woods.

June Bug had settled in for about 40 minutes when he heard the dogs start baying and barking. Midnight and Fluffy were older dogs, but had more bark and June Bug could tell from their bark they were onto something. Butch would be leading the chase because he was younger. A lot of times, the older dogs would give out and would head back home or go to the truck while Butch would keep up the chase for hours. From the sound of the dogs, the deer was cutting back and forth across the creek that ran not far from June Bug's stand. Sure enough, a deer came running hard down by the stream. June Bug knew it would be a tough shot-the deer running like it was. As the deer got within range, June Bug saw it was a doe and today wasn't doe day. Shooting a doe on a non-doe day was a serious offense, almost as bad a shining. So, June Bug sat helplessly as he watched Butch chase the doe off downstream.

June Bug climbed down out of the stand and started walking out of the woods when the two older dogs came up to him panting and slobbering. They were worn out and would have let him carry them home. He called Butch a couple of times, but he knew Butch would run for a long time before he would get anything like tuckered out. He would come home late and be on the porch in the morning, so June Bug started the trudge back to the truck. When he got there, Daddy was waiting.

"See anything?"

"Yea, big doe was all. Butch was on her pretty hard, so he won't be back for a while."

"Well," his daddy said, "we didn't get any game, but it is sure good to be out of doors on a day like this." Daddy could tell June Bug was frustrated and wanted to cheer him up. June Bug would not be cheered. It was a perfect day for hunting and nothing is more wonderful than a crisp, fall day. But June Bug was sullen over seeing two deer and not getting a shot.

When they got back to the house CB was there waiting. CB got his nickname from talking like a trucker. While he managed to break that habit he never really got over the nickname. "CB, how are you?" June Bug's daddy asked.

"I'm fine, Mr. Deroy. Y'all have any luck today?"

"Didn't get any game, but it was a good day to be out." Turning to June Bug, "Son, you going back to hunt the stand this evening?"

"Naw, Sir, the dogs have chased anything out, won't be much use."

"Suit yourself."

"Can me and CB go do something?"

"Well," his daddy paused. It seemed like every time those boys went off there was a fair chance of trouble joining them. Nothing serious, they just seemed to draw the stupid out of each other. "If your gun is clean, you won't get into trouble, you mind your manners, and if it is okay by your mama, yea, you can go. And make sure you are home by 10:30, not 10:31."

"Yes, Daddy. Didn't shoot nothing so I don't need to clean the gun. I'll go ask mama." June Bug said to his daddy and to CB.

So, a few minutes later, CB and June Bug were riding in CB's rattletrap truck talking about the one that got away and the frustrations of hunting.

CB pops his mouth off, "You want a deer? I can get you a deer."

"Yea, how you going to do that? Got one in your back pocket you're goin' to pull out?" June Bug knew that CB was a lot of talk when it came to hunting. He wasn't patient, quiet or steady-three things you need if you are going to be any good at hunting.

"There are ways to get a deer and there are ways to get a deer. You only know about half of 'em".

"What you talking about CB? I forgot more about hunting today than you know."

CB just sat behind the wheel of the truck and smiled real big. "What if I told you I was part of a hunting club and we never get skunked? We always get a deer!"

June Bug didn't say anything for a long time. He could not imagine that CB had a secret about hunting that he didn't know about. But if there was something out there that might improve his chances when hunting, he wanted to know what it was. "What do you do?"

CB just smiled and sat real quiet. If C.B. was quiet, which was real hard for him, it had to be important. Finally, CB could hold it in no longer, "We go shining," he said real proud.

"You, what?! You know if they catch you, you could end up in jail! CB, you're crazy!"

"We won't get caught. Earl Watson calls the game warden from a pay phone in town and he says that somebody is shining up near Duck Creek Swamp. While the game warden is up on the north side of the county we go someplace south. Sometimes we have a deer in less than 10 minutes, put it in the bed of a truck and off we go. One time there was a whole bunch of us going, so we hooked up a trailer full of hay to a truck and acted like we were on a hayride. That night we shot two deer and hid them under the hay. No game warden is going to stop a hay ride."

"Where you clean and dress it?"

"We take it out to Earl Watson's. He has a place where he butchers it."

"I ain't going nowhere near any of them no-count Watson's, especially at night." June Bug said then changed the subject, "Let's go get something to eat."

June Bug had the feeling he ought to have CB take him home right away. It seemed that CB was getting closer to the Watson's and that was always a bad thing. CB's mama was not a Watson, but her brother married a girl, who had a sister that was married to a boy that had a cousin that was married to a Watson. That didn't strictly make CB a Watson but it made him distant kin, which was bad enough. But instead of going back to June Bug's house they drove over CB's, ate sandwiches and started watching some football. Both teams were Yankee schools, so the boys weren't real interested.

When it was close to dark, June Bug told CB that he needed to go home. They got in the truck and headed toward June Bug's house. "Tell you what, June Bug," CB said as they rode along. "Why don't we swing by that soybean field other side of the woods from where your daddy keeps his cows? I'll spotlight a deer for you.

"Don't suppose it will do any harm to just look at em', do you?" CB continued to his reluctant friend.

"Naw, I don't guess it'll hurt just to look," June Bug said. He was more interested than he was letting on.

Deroy kept a few head of cattle in a pasture out back of the house. Beyond that pasture was a thick woods where June Bug would hunt and on the other side of that woods was a soybean field. June Bug knew that the deer that sheltered in the woods would feed in the field during the night. So, when CB suggested spotlighting that field he figured there would be a whole herd of deer out there. Beans had been harvested a while back, but the deer would still be picking up the gleanings.

They pulled off the road by the field and C.B. eased out of the truck and set up a spotlight on the hood of his truck. He began sweeping the field with the white beam of light. First couple of passes didn't reveal anything. But the third time across, a pair of amber eyes were looking back glowing in the night. June Bug was standing in the bed of the truck and he whispered down to C.B., "That's a small deer." When he looked down, CB was getting his rifle out. "CB, don't you shoot that deer, it is too small!"

"He is bigger than a bean and you would eat a bean." CB was stretching out over the hood of the truck. Every now and then, the eyes would disappear for a second, but then would reappear. CB whispered out loud, "There he is." June Bug started to yell hoping it would scare the deer off. But his voice was lost in the roar of the rifle's report and the eyes vanished.

"Let's go see what I got!" CB was elated. He hung the rifle in the gun rack and tossed the light on the floorboard. He drove across the stubble toward the carcass in the field. The truck jumped and jolted and came to a spot a few feet from the lifeless form. He jumped out and ran up and stopped. June Bug came around the truck and nothing could have prepared him for what he saw. It was Butch, dead as a doorknob, with a bullet hole just over his right eye.

"You shot my dog, you stupid, jackass! That's my dog!" And June Bug bent down to grab Butch and began to cry and cry really hard. CB mumbled something about being sorry, but just mostly stood feeling pretty bad himself. After a few moments, June Bug stood up, looked at CB and said, "If I had a gun I might just shoot you. As it is if you are standing there in 10 seconds, I will beat the life out of you." CB saw that June Bug meant it and realized that shooting someone's dog is a great way to get beaten bad.

"June Bug, you know ...."

"One, two, three ...."

By seven, CB was in the truck and leaving fast. It was a long and painful walk home even cutting across the pasture. When June Bug walked in the house, he scared his mama to death. June Bug had blood on his hands, shirt, and face. "I am okay, Mama. CB shot Butch; this is his blood." Grandpa Lymon who had come over to supper raised an eyebrow, which for him was a display of extreme emotion.

Deroy got hot fast, not caring much for CB in the best of time, "What the Sam Hill was that boy doing?"

"It is a long story, Daddy. I need to go bury him," he paused. "Butch, not CB. Can I get the truck keys?"

"I'll go with you, Son," Grandpa Lymon said. On the drive June Bug related the whole story. Grandpa Lymon just listened and let June Bug be mad. After he told about threatening to kill CB, June Bug concluded with, "I ain't going to kill him, but I am never speaking to him again and he best steer clear of me." June Bug drove slow and quiet for a moment. "Got any wise words for me, Grandpa?"

"When we break the law sooner or later someone gets hurt. Careless shootin' like CB was doing can get people killed. That is why we have laws. When people disregard laws, even if they think they know what they are doing, they put other people or their property at risk. That is why the Proverbs say, 'Whoso despiseth the word shall be destoried, but he that fearth the commandment shall be rewarded.' Sooner or later those boys out shining are going to suffer for it, but in the meantime, others also have to pay the consequences."

As they stood beside Butch's grave June Bug asked, "Grandpa, is it wrong to pray over a dog's grave?"

"Naw, as a matter of fact, I was going to pray," and he did. He prayed for June Bug and CB and the Watson's and for justice.

Turns out that Grandpa Lymon was a bit of a prophet. The boys doing the shining did suffer for it. Someone called the game warden and suggested that if he got an anonymous tip about shining on one side of the county that he ought to ease over to the other side of the county. A couple of weeks later, six of the Watson's and their close kin had some explaining to do. CB and June Bug never became friends again, but CB learned his lesson, and for his part, June Bug didn't kill him.

CHAPTER 20

June Bug Always Has a Pig Named Lucy

From the time they started dating, everyone was pretty sure June Bug was going to marry Beth Ann. They were close before they started dating and their families were really close. Once they started dating, things went steadily along toward the marriage altar. However, there was one occasion when there was some doubt, not on the part of Beth Ann and June Bug, but amongst some other folks. And it has to do with why June Bug, to this very day, keeps at least one hog named Lucy. As stories go, it came and went in pretty short order. From Thursday night till Sunday was as long as it took. It was the only time that anyone ever tried to bust up June Bug and Beth Ann.

There was a girl at Robert Frost High by the name of Lucy Dilton. Lucy was a girl that was easy to look at for all the wrong reasons. She was pretty with curly, blond hair, deep blue eyes, a pretty smile, and a flirtatious personality. Lucy liked all the boys, at least as long as they were around, and held no compunction about flirting with a boy who had a steady girlfriend. Lucy wore clothes that would attract attention. When the *Dukes of Hazzard* was a weekly TV show, Lucy tried her best to make her wardrobe look like Daisy Duke's outfits. On more than one occasion, she was sent home from school to change her clothes. Beyond what she wore, she had a bad reputation concerning her morals. This was a time when to say a girl was 'easy' was to question her very character. Lucy was said to be very easy.

In the spring of her junior year of high school, Lucy set her cap for June Bug (to "set your cap" for someone was an old hunting term that came from setting a percussion cap on the rifle nipple just before you shot the game). June Bug had no interest in Lucy, but was polite to her. The combination of his unavailability and politeness caused Lucy to chase June Bug hard.

Every year during Easter break (called spring break now days) the choir from Robert Frost High would go on a weekend tour. The choir would practice all spring and then perform a concert on Thursday night at one of the local churches then leave to go on a mini tour. They would sing Friday night and twice on Saturday and twice on Sunday. They generally got home late Sunday night to be ready for the next week of school. This year Beth Ann had a solo in one of the numbers. It was while Beth Ann was away on this concert tour that Lucy decided that she would do her darnedest to get June Bug.

All spring Lucy had been flirting with June Bug and her advances were not unnoticed by folks. Beth Ann was not a jealous sort, but she was getting to where she didn't care much for Lucy. June Bug's mama and daddy didn't say a thing, but there was the feeling they didn't like that girl much either. The only person who ever said anything about Lucy was Grandpa Lymon.

Grandpa Lymon was never heard to say a bad thing about anyone, except maybe the no-count, white trash Watson's or Tennessee Vols fans. In fact, he was the kind of old man that women loved to be around 'cause he liked to tell them how pretty they were. Caroline called him the 'oldest flirt' in the county. He was a charmer as an old man. Except when it came to Lucy. All he would say to her, excepting business talk at the store, was a cross between snort and growl. He did not like her at all, but was re-strained by his Southern upbringing in what he would actually say.

Thursday night just before the concert, Beth Ann was in the back of the church with the choir and June Bug was sitting by himself in the second pew waiting for Grandpa Lymon to arrive. Grandpa Lymon sat in the same pew from the day the church built that new building. One time somebody spoke to him smart-aleck-like, "I see you're sitting in your pew." Grandpa responded saucily, "Humph, I don't smell nothing." June Bug knew exactly what seat Grandpa would come to when he came in, so he took a seat and waited for Grandpa to arrive.

Who should show up, but Lucy? She was dressed fit to kill wearing a tight, black dress that was not nearly long enough. She walked up to June Bug and said, "Deroy, can I sit with you tonight?" Before he could say a word she sat down right next to June Bug. She was sitting so close he could feel her pressing up against him real tight. About a minute later, Grandpa Ly-mon walked up, looked at the two of them-June Bug pressed up against the arm rest on one side and Lucy hard on the other-and said, "Scoot over, young lady, that is where I sit. Besides, you should leave room for the Holy Spirit. He could not have gotten between you two." There was no twinkle in his eye; no humor in his voice. Lucy slid over enough for Grandpa Lymon to put himself between June Bug and Lucy.

The concert was a great success. The choir did great every year, but this year it seemed, at least to June Bug, that the choir outdid itself and every other choir in the world. When Beth Ann got up to sing, June Bug was convinced that she was the greatest singer who ever sang. When the concert was over and every-one was applauding and the soloists were taking their bows, June Bug didn't notice that Lucy wasn't clapping. But, Grandpa Lymon noticed.

Later that evening in the church parking lot the kids from the choir said their goodbyes and loaded on the bus for the drive up to Nashville where they would be singing Friday evening. No sooner was the bus out of the parking lot than Lucy came up to June Bug and said, "Deroy, can you give me a ride home? I don't want to trouble my parents and it is too far to walk." Everyone knew that Lucy didn't mind causing her parents trouble and it was only a couple of blocks to her house, but June Bug the Southern gentleman courteously offered the services of his pickup. When they get over to the truck, sitting in the middle of the seat was Grandpa Lymon. It would seem that he had been paying close attention to Lucy's contrivances.

"Grandpa, what you doin' here?"

"I need you to give me a ride."

"I was going to take Lucy home."

"Humph, that's fine. You take me where I want to go after we drop her off."

So, the three of them drove two blocks with Grandpa Lymon sitting between them in the front seat.

"Deroy, whatcha doing tomorrow?"

"He is helping me at the store." Grandpa said.

"Well, I may stop by to say 'hi' while you work," Lucy said none too happy that Grandpa was getting in her way.

"While he is working he hasn't time for visiting, so don't waste your time."

June Bug was stunned. He had never heard Grandpa Lymon being so curt and harsh with anyone, especially not a young lady. Generally, he treated teenage girls like they were some kind of queen.

"Well, here we are." June Bug slowed the truck to a stop.

"Walk me to the door, Deroy?" Lucy was working hard to overcome the curmudgeon that Grandpa Lymon had become.

"Naw, I need to get on home and Grandpa needs to talk to me about something."

Once they pulled away June Bug started, "Grandpa, I have never in my life seen you anything like rude, but you were sure being hard on Lucy tonight."

"Son, that girl is wicked. I hear a lot around the store and many times it's things I don't want to hear; many sad reports. I am telling you that girl is trouble. She will wreck you and Beth Ann and not care one bit the hurt she causes and then leave you behind like a horse biscuit on the trail."

"Grandpa, I ain't going to let nothing happen to me and Beth Ann. I am just being polite to Lucy. I don't care one bit for her."

"That is the point, boy! She will eat at you little by little and bad will come of it. You figure out how to keep her away. I care about you and I think the world of Beth Ann and I've lived long enough to know what is what. You mind me, Son."

June Bug spent that Friday with Grandpa Lymon at the store. He didn't do a lot of work; just the general presence of a shopkeeper. Just before closing time and in spite of Grandpa Lymon's prohibition, Lucy drove up in her daddy's car. She was dressed in a plaid, blue shirt that was unbuttoned to the third button and tied at the waist. She had on shorts that were so skimpy you would find more cotton in an aspirin bottle than in those clothes.

"Hey, June Bug, me and some friends are going to my family's lake house tomorrow. You want to come?" She smiled a big smile and gave a little wink that made June Bug wonder who, if anyone, from Lucy's family was going to be there.

"Thanks, Lucy, but I've got some chores on the farm I got to take care of." At this point a countenance of great contentment settled on Grandpa Lymon. But it disappeared like frost in the sunshine when June Bug continued, "But it would be great to have you come out to Grandpa's to eat lunch with us on Sunday after church. Isn't that right, Grandpa?" There was a cloud on Grandpa Lymon's face that settled into a scowl.

"Well, we will call it a date." Lucy replied as she turned around flipping her hair in all directions while she walked out.

About a minute later, June Bug went over to the counter and said, "Grandpa, I want to buy one of those little rings you keep in the knickknack shelf."

"What do you need one of them for?" Grandpa asked.

"I'm going to give it to Lucy."

Before Grandpa would say a word June Bug looked up at him and said, "It is okay, Grandpa, I know what I am a doing."

June Bug spent Saturday working on the farm. Grandpa had a few head of stock as did Deroy Sr., but this day June Bug was fixing up the hog lot. He had just got a sow and was going to raise feeder pigs to make a little extra money. In addition to fixing the lot, he and his daddy were going to have to ring the sow and that was a two-man job. By the end of the day's chores he was too tired to go out, so when Lucy called that evening he just promised to see her at church the next day.

Nobody was really happy about having Lucy to lunch. Deroy Sr. knew her daddy and didn't care for him much. Caroline was the model of Southern grace, but not far under the skin, she was boiling. Grandpa sounded like an old steam engine with all the huffing and puffing he was doing. Only June Bug seemed at peace and that bothered the rest of them more than anything. When church was over they all headed out to Grandpa's for lunch. Grandpa drove June Bug's little brother and sister, but June Bug and Lucy rode in the back of the family AMC Matador. It was deathly quiet till Lucy leaned over to rest her head on June Bug's shoulder. Her head no more touched him, than Caroline said, "Sit up, Lucy, you can't be that tired." The rest of the drive was abnormally quiet for what is generally a chatty family.

Once to the house, Caroline started getting things on the table. Deroy Sr. was a helping, Grandpa Lymon sat down with the Sunday paper and Lucy sat down too; never even offering to help. Well, June Bug's mama was about to say something when June Bug said, "Lucy, I want to show you something. Come with me."

Grandpa Lymon piped up, "I'll go too." Lucy rolled her eyes and sighed deeply, but got up to go with June Bug.

June Bug took Lucy up to the hog lot and said, "I wanted to show you my new sow. What do you think of her?"

"Deroy, that is disgusting! I don't want to look at your stupid pig. Let's go do something fun." At this point, Lucy was somewhere between giving June Bug the big lip treatment and losing her temper.

"But Lucy..." June Bug's voice became earnest, "I wanted you to see her. I named her after you." Lucy was stunned, not sure if she should be insulted or, in some county-hick way, flattered. "In fact, yesterday when daddy and me wrung her nose I put one of those dime store, costume jewelry rings on her ringer. It is covered in dirt, but if you look real close you can see it. You see, Lucy, you remind me of that sow."

At this point, Grandpa Lymon made a sound that was somewhere between a gasp, a chuckle and the sound an asthmatic chicken might make as it died. Lucy, for her part, could not comprehend what June Bug just said. Either that or she was too stunned to speak because she didn't say a word.

June Bug continued, "Proverbs is my favorite book in the Bible and it says in Proverbs, 'As a jewel of gold in a swine's snout, so is a fair woman which is without discretion.' You see, Lucy, you are a very pretty girl, almost as pretty as Beth Ann. But you throw yourself at every guy who comes along and the talk is you are not a lady on a date. I know we will never be friends after this, but you need someone to tell you the truth."

It was at that moment that Lucy's fangs came out. She called June Bug everything but a white boy. Cussed him like she was a sailor or maybe even a Marine and told him what he could do with his pig, the Book of Proverbs and his whole family. What she told him to do is quite impossible. Then she took off and said she was going to walk home. Caroline heard the ruckus and came out to see what was going on. She got her keys and convinced

Lucy to let her give her a ride home. Caroline reported that it was very quiet in the car the whole time.

Grandpa Lymon took June Bug aside and said, "Son, you don't believe in half measures do you? You know she is going to do everything she can to make your life miserable, don't you?"

"Yes, Sir, but I couldn't think of any other way to tell her. Nobody else will tell her. She is loose and I just wanted to be clear about my opinion."

Rumor spread all over high school that June Bug asked Lucy to marry him and that she turned him down and that is why they were not speaking to each other. Since Lucy was the only one spreading that rumor nobody believed it much. Beth Ann heard it and June Bug said she should ask Grandpa Lymon. She asked Grandpa Lymon what happened and he just laughed and said you had to be there. And no one ever talked about that lunch again.

Lucy never said a nice word to or about June Bug ever again. She went away to college after graduation. Not long after, her folks moved away and no one heard a word from her for years. Then on the day June Bug and Beth Ann got married, she showed up at the church house. After the wedding, when Beth Ann Johnson was receiving their guests and shaking hands with everybody, Lucy walked up and gave Beth Ann a hug and said, "Tell Deroy I took the ring out." Then she left.

"What does that mean, Deroy?" Beth Ann asked later.

"I'm not completely sure, but I think it is good news."

To this day Deroy, who now lives on the family farm and has a son named Tadpole, always names one of his hogs Lucy.

About the Author

Charles (Charlie) Crowe believes that the best moments in life are always good stories. Even the worst moments in life come to us as the stories we hear or the story we live. He loves to tell and to hear good stories. Starting when he was only four years old, on trips to visit his Granny Bell, he always insisted on having a joke to tell her. Growing up in a preacher's home there was constantly a story going on. Charlie was not a particularly good student because he discovered that daydreaming is more interesting than classroom work. He can vividly remember daydreams from first grade. One day he got into trouble daydreaming about a heroic fight with a giant spider, which was much more interesting that whatever was going on in the classroom at the moment.

During his ministry, Charlie consistently tried to communicate the greatest story ever told by means of stories. Beyond the discipline of hermeneutics and exegeses he loved to share the story of scripture. As a church consultant, he still uses the power of story as a way to teach what churches should do and what they need to avoid.

Charlie's children grew up on the oddity of Theodore Rex Lizard, aka Teddy the Wonder Lizard, from the planet Zortron who managed to appear at bedtime, the dinner table, and even at birthday parties for children too old for stories.

He firmly believes that if you can get people to tell you their story and listen to your story you will most likely become friends.

On his tombstone there may well be Charlie's trademark quote, "That reminds me of a story...."